SPACE QUEST

Herbie Brennan is a professional writer whose work has appeared in more than fifty countries. He began a career in journalism at the age of eighteen and when he was twenty-four became the youngest newspaper editor in his native Ireland.

By his mid-twenties, he had published his first novel, an historical romance brought out by Doubleday in New York. At age thirty, he made the decision to devote his time to full-length works of fiction for both adults and children. Since then he has published more than ninety books, many of them international best-sellers, for both adults and children.

Other books by Herbie Brennan
published by Faber & Faber

The Spy's Handbook

SPACE QUEST

111 peculiar questions
about the universe and beyond

Herbie Brennan

Illustrated by The Maltings

faber and faber

ILLUSTRATED BY THE MALTINGS

First published in 2003 by Faber and Faber Limited
3 Queen Square, London WC1N 3AU

Typeset by Faber and Faber Limited
Printed in England by Bookmarque Ltd.

© Herbie Brennan, 2003

Herbie Brennan is hereby identified as author of this work in
accordance with Section 77 of the Copyright, Designs and Patents
Act 1988

A CIP record for this book is available from the British Library

ISBN 0-571-21673 0

2 4 6 8 10 9 7 5 3 1

Contents

To my dear niece and nephew, Lotte and Kit, who are stars in their own right. With much love.

Introduction

You know how it is. You wake up one morning and all you can think about is what would happen if you fell into a Black Hole that day? Or you start to wonder what's outside the universe? Or how big a collision it would take to make the Earth explode? Or why wizards always have stars embroidered on their hats?

Fear not. The answers are at hand. Right here in this book, in fact, along with just about every other peculiar question you've ever thought of asking about space, stars, planets or little green men.

The whole thing is divided into convenient sections so you know where to look for the question you want to ask (or one like it). What's more, there's a quiz at the end of each section, so you can track the astonishing amount of knowledge you've accumulated and discover whether you should grade yourself Useless Worm or Master of the Universe.

So gird your loins – privately, please – because here comes the first question…

1 How big is the universe?

Very. Very, very. Very, very, very big. It's so big it makes no sense to think in kilometres or miles, so scientists talk about something called light years.

Light travels approximately 300,000 kilometres (186,000 miles) every *second*. That's 18,000,000 kilometres (11,185,200 miles) a minute, 1,080,000,000 kilometres (6,711,120 miles) an hour, 24,920,000,000 kilometres (15,485,288,000 miles) a day. Which means a light year – the distance light travels in the course of a year – is 9,095,800,000,000 kilometres (5,651,800,000,000 miles) long.

Our nearest star (apart from the sun) is 4.3 light years away. The most distant star shines in a galaxy literally billions of light years away. And that's only the bit of the universe we can detect. Beyond that there's almost certainly more universe.

So the honest answer to your 'how big' question is we don't know exactly. But it's as big as you can imagine, plus a bit more.

2 How do you measure the universe?

You examine the light coming from the farthest object you can find.

If something is moving away from you really far and really fast, the light coming from it gets more and more red. In astronomy, this is known – sensibly enough – as the red shift.

An American astronomer named Edwin Powell Hubble discovered that light from distant galaxies showed a red shift. The greater the red shift, the farther away the object was and the faster it was travelling.

Hubble quickly realised that you could use this fact to make measurements and worked out a formula, now known as Hubble's Law, which is the basis of modern calculations about the size of the universe.

3 Is there anything outside it?

Very good question. It's difficult to imagine a universe that goes on forever, but just as difficult to get your brain around one that is complete in itself with nothing outside it, even if the 'nothing' is just empty space.

In the early years of the twentieth century, Albert Einstein, who produced two excellent theories of the universe, suggested it might be 'finite but boundless,' thus adding something else impossible to imagine. More recently, cosmic scientists have suggested there isn't just one universe, but a vast collection of them floating like bubbles in some sort of hyperspace.

So is there anything outside the universe?

Yes … no … probably … sort of … maybe …

Next question please.

4 What's a Black Hole?

It's the corpse of a very large star.

5 Is it really black?

Funnily enough it's violet. A Black Hole sucks in light, which definitely means it has a black heart – as black as it could possibly get, in fact. But even Black Hole gravity doesn't stretch forever. Right at the edge, on the border between normal space and the area where light is drawn in, sub-atomic particles become highly charged and glow violet. So from the outside, that's the colour of a Black Hole.

You don't want to know how it looks from the inside.

6 Are Black Holes just theory or have astronomers actually found one?

There are a couple of things you look for when you're hunting a Black Hole. One is lots of X-rays. A Black Hole sucks in every atom and particle in its neighbourhood and speeds them up so they give out radiation. Much of this radiation is in the form of X-rays, so if you find an area of space generating huge amounts of X-rays, you can start to suspect there's a Black Hole in there somewhere.

The other thing you look for is massive gravity. Black Holes are the greatest gravity generators in the universe. If there happens to be a visible star in the same area, it will be influenced by the gravity field. You might see it being drawn into orbit, or parts of its substance might be sucked away. The star might even be swallowed whole.

In 1970, astronomers picked up one of these signs in the constellation Cygnus, where something was generating a million times more radiation than our sun. Then they found a blue supergiant star was orbiting the source. With the two signs in place, they concluded they were studying an actual Black Hole, the first one ever found. Since then, signs of Black Holes have turned up in more than a hundred areas of space and astronomers have no doubt many more are still waiting to be discovered.

7 What would happen if I fell into a Black Hole?

Nothing very pleasant and something very strange indeed. The tiny difference in gravity between your head and your feet would be enough to ensure you were stretched out into a tall, thin creature thousands of kilometres long and just a few atoms thick. A very *dead* tall, thin creature, that is...

But from another point of view, it will never happen. One of the peculiarities of a Black Hole is that its gravity is strong enough to distort time. Scientists calculate that if they watched you falling into a Black Hole, your descent would get slower and slower until you eventually came to a halt. This is because time itself would be slowing down as you moved closer to the Black Hole until that magical moment when it stopped altogether.

Once time stopped, you would hang frozen like a fly in amber, not thinking, not moving, not getting any older, for ever and ever. Would you still be alive when that happened? It's difficult to say, because while you wouldn't be dead either, things like life and death don't make much sense around a Black Hole. Nor does anything else really.

If I were you, I'd try not to fall into one at all.

8 How do you make a Black Hole?

There's been some talk of trying to create miniature Black Holes in the laboratory, but it hasn't happened yet. So unless some advanced alien civilization has been at work, the only Black Holes in the universe are made by nature. Here's how it happens.

When a star gets old and uses up its fuel, different things can happen. It can simply burn out, leaving a miserable husk. Or it can go nova and blow up a bit, or go supernova and blow up completely, leaving nothing at all behind.

With a big star – something between 1.4 and 2 times the size of our sun – the most usual thing is for it to collapse under its own weight, growing smaller and more densely packed until it becomes a neutron star. A neutron star can actually be smaller than a planet – maybe as little as 20 kilometres (12^1/$_2$ miles) in diameter – but it makes up for its size in sheer density, which is more than a million, million times greater than water. That makes it so heavy a single spoonful of neutron star stuff would weigh a thousand million tonnes.

But if a star is bigger still – more than three times larger than our sun – the collapse continues past the neutron star stage. The star gets smaller and smaller, heavier and heavier, until, like something out of *Alice in Wonderland,* it disappears altogether.

Leaving behind a Black Hole.

9 What's an Event Horizon?

At the point of ultimate collapse, the dying star reaches zero volume and infinite density – something scientists call the singularity. You can't see the singularity (which is the centre of the Black Hole) because it's hidden by a sort of surface called the event horizon.

The event horizon marks the point where the escape velocity of the Black Hole (the speed something has to travel to overcome the gravity of an astronomical body) is greater than the speed of light. Once you pass the event horizon, there's no turning back for anything, including light itself, which is why the whole thing was called a Black Hole in the first place.

You can actually work out where the event horizon will be, thanks to the efforts of a German astronomer named Karl Schwarzschild. He calculated that the radius of an event horizon depended on the mass of the collapsing star. If the star was l0 times larger than our sun, for example, the event horizon would be only 30 kilometres (18$^1/_2$ miles) from the core.

10 Is space empty?

Not even slightly. Although Outer Space – the area of space beyond our solar system – is often described by astronomers as an almost perfect vacuum, that word 'almost' is important. It would be difficult, if not impossible, to find an area of space that did not contain at least a few particles of dust and an abundance of cosmic rays.

11 When did the universe start?

Best estimates run between 10,000,000,000 and 15,000,000,000 years ago, according to Big Bang Theory. Our solar system is a lot newer.

12 What's Big Bang Theory?

It's the theory most astronomers currently believe about how the universe got started.

According to this theory, everything began with a single lump of hugely compressed and very hot something – you can't call it matter since time, space, energy and a few other things were all compressed in there as well – which suddenly 'expanded rapidly.'

The result of this rapid expansion (a polite way of describing a massive explosion) was that things became less densely packed and cooled down a bit. Processes started that left the universe with more matter in it than anti-matter and further cooling allowed the appearance of hydrogen, helium and lithium, although only in nucleus form. After about a million years, atoms started to form and radiation travelled through space. (You can still detect that original radiation today, as two physicists, Arno A. Penzias and Robert W. Wilson, discovered in 1965.)

There's a bit more to the details, but that's about the bones of it. Somewhere between 10,000 and 15,000 million years ago, everything was squeezed together in a single ball which exploded into the universe we know and love today. We don't know what was there before the ball and since time only appeared as part of the Big Bang you can't really talk about 'before' anyway. And we don't know what the ball expanded into, because space didn't exist before the Big Bang either.

13 Why did it go off?

Nobody knows.

14 Did it make a lot of noise?

It didn't make any. To make a noise, you have to generate sound waves. Sound waves can only travel in air, water or some similar carrier medium. No carrier, no sound.

Did you know?

Before the Big Bang occurred, there was neither space nor time, consequently nothing that could have carried sound. It may have been the most brutally violent event in the history of the universe, but it happened so quietly you could have heard a pin drop.

15 When will time stop?

Time's a lot more tricky than you'd think. The best joke ever made about this goes: *Time flies like an arrow. Fruit flies like a banana.* Because while time *seems* to fly like an arrow, always pointing away from the past and towards the future, it isn't *really* like an arrow at all.

Back in the early years of the twentieth century, the great scientist Albert Einstein showed time was actually part of space and thus subject to the same sort of physical laws. One of those laws is that time is influenced by gravity – the more gravity there is, the more slowly time runs.

You won't notice this effect standing anywhere on Earth. There's just not enough gravity about. You wouldn't even notice it on a high gravity planet like Jupiter or Saturn, for the same reason. But when you start to consider the massive gravity of really large stars, it's a different story. Here the slowing down of time becomes measurable, at least by calculation.

Something else that influences time is speed. The minute you start moving, time slows. The faster you move, the more it slows. You won't notice this effect either if you're walking the dog or even riding in an express train. Time slows all right, but not enough to measure. But you can measure it in an aeroplane. Indeed, scientists proved this part of Einstein's Relativity Theory by flying a super-accurate atomic clock around the world, then comparing it with a second atomic clock that stayed on the ground. The tiny fraction of a second difference showed time had indeed slowed down, if only just a little.

Where this gets interesting is when you start to consider a tiny particle, smaller than an atom, called the muon. Muons zip around at 99% the speed of light. Scientists calculated that if you had a spaceship powered by muons, time on board would run seven times slower than time outside. Einstein gave some idea what this would mean when he constructed what he called his Twins Paradox.

Did you know?

If you're unfortunate enough to get caught up in the gravitational field of a Black Hole it will slow down time so much that it stops altogether. Some scientists – like the mathematician Kurt Gödel – calculate that a Black Hole could actually make time run backwards.

The Twins Paradox starts with identical twins, one of whom becomes the captain of a muon-powered spaceship, while the other stays at home to feed the dog. The twins are 30 years old when the astronaut twin sets off on a five-year mission to explore the galaxy. By the time he gets back, he's 35 years old.

But since his spaceship was travelling at 99% the speed of light, time inside was passing seven times more slowly than time on Earth. So the twin he left behind has aged by 35 years. You can see why Einstein called it a paradox. You're now stuck with twins one of whom is 35 while the other is 65 years old.

Now suppose you put a supercharger on the spaceship. Instead of travelling at muon speed, its light-speed percentage pushes up from 99 to 99.1 ... 99.2 ... 99.3 ... and so on until it starts to cruise at fully 100% the speed of light. At that point, time will stop.

Albert Einstein

But that's only the time inside the spaceship, of course. If you're interested in when *all* time will stop, you have to consider the fate of the universe. Most scientists now believe the universe began in a single tightly packed ball that exploded at the time of the Big Bang and has been expanding ever since. It may be that the universe will keep expanding until everything is so stretched apart and thinned that matter as we know it ceases to exist and all motion stops. At that point, time stops as well, for all practical purposes.

Without change, there's nothing by which you can measure or experience time.

But there is another possibility. Before the universe runs down completely, gravity may start it shrinking again. From then on, it will be like running a movie backwards. The universe will get smaller and smaller until it compacts into the sort of ball you had when it started. At that point, time will stop.

Unless, of course, there's a second Big Bang, in which case I confidently expect it to start up again.

16 How cold is space?

If you keep away from stars, it hits absolute zero, which is -273.15° Celsius or -459.67° Fahrenheit.

17 What shape is it?

According to Einstein, it's curved.

I know that doesn't make much sense, but you have to look at space the way Einstein did when he was working on his famous Theories of Relativity. He'd reached the stage where he'd decided space and time weren't separate, but parts of a single thing he called spacetime (or sometimes the spacetime continuum). The trouble was he couldn't imagine what spacetime looked like. It made no sense in terms of the geometry he had been taught at school.

The geometry taught at school was worked out by a Greek called Euclid, who was born in 320 BCE. Euclid grew up to become a schoolteacher in Alexandria in Egypt and at some stage of his career wrote a book

called *Elements*. You may never
have read *Elements*, but if you
learned geometry at school you
know what was in it.

Euclid

Euclid started with the idea
that it's obvious you can only
draw one line parallel to a
given line through a given
point. From there he worked
out the whole foundations of
geometry as we know it. He
worked out that the three
angles of a triangle always
add up to 180 degrees. He
worked out that the square on
the hypotenuse is equal to the
sum of the squares on the other two sides. He worked out
that the circumference of a circle is $2\pi r$. And so on and
so on. Most people imagine this is the only geometry
there could possibly be. Not so.

Did you know?

*The basis of the geometry we all take for
granted has never actually been proved.
Not anywhere. Not ever.*

As long ago as the nineteenth century, a few
mathematicians started to wonder what would happen if
Euclid's basic idea about the parallel line and the point
was simply wrong. He hadn't proved it after all – he'd
just said it was obvious. So they developed two new

geometries with different starting points. One was called hyperbolic geometry and it was based on the idea that you could draw two or more lines parallel to a given line through a given point. The other was called elliptic geometry and that was based on the idea that you couldn't draw any lines parallel to a given line through a given point.

While Einstein was struggling to make sense of spacetime, somebody suggested his problem might be he was using the wrong geometry. Euclid's geometry works so well on Earth we tend to think it must be the same everywhere. But suppose it isn't? Suppose there are certain situations where Euclid's geometry doesn't work at all?

It was an interesting idea, so Einstein tried applying other geometries to his problem. To his delight, he found elliptic geometry worked perfectly. And elliptic geometry told him space had to be curved. In fact, the whole of space had to be a sphere.

18 Where does God live?

In the old days, people generally thought heaven – God's traditional home – was somewhere up in the sky. (We still refer to the night sky as 'the heavens.') But as scientists learned more and more about the real nature of the universe, this idea became less popular. Space probes, moon shots and robot landings on other planets more or less scotched it completely.

But there are still plenty of other possibilities. One is that God is actually the totality of everything and consequently lives everywhere at once. Another is that heaven exists in another dimension of reality. Another is that God was – and is – the Great Void out of which the universe sprang at the time of the Big Bang. Another is that heaven is a state rather than a place, something that lies deep in your mind, rather than the distant reaches of Outer Space.

So where does God live? Wherever He wants – She's God, right?

19 How will the universe end?

Not with a bang, but with a whimper, according to the poet T. S. Eliot. Scientists aren't quite so certain. There are several schools of thought about how the universe may end, based on the theory – accepted by a majority of scientists – that the universe is currently expanding. Here's how one scenario might look if you were able to watch it.

Long after our solar system is no more, the galaxies themselves will begin to burn out. As they disappear, the universe as a whole will take on a different look. The great star clusters will be fewer and more spread out. Dust clouds, left behind by galactic collapses, will be spreading so widely that they begin to obscure the stars that are left.

As the matter of the universe thins out and spreads, there is a likelihood of increasing collisions with antimatter, creating vast explosions of energy. As this energy is absorbed by the enormous dust clouds, the temperature of the entire universe will begin to rise. Eventually the dust will begin to glow.

Since the universe is still expanding, the few remaining galaxies will be out of sight of one another by now and vast reaches of the universe will be filled with the huge, hot clouds. This, then, is the heat death of the universe. But even in this scenario, the universe can get more dead still.

Given enough time, the vast reserves of energy generated by the Big Bang will begin to run out. Expansion of the universe will slow. With so much of the original universe pulverised into dust, gravity begins to weaken and the whole continuum of spacetime loses its distinctive shape.

The old, turbulent energies will eventually achieve a state of balance. Nothing more will happen. Nothing more *can* happen. Everything is still. The universe has ended.

But maybe the forces of gravity will prove strong enough to stop the expansion before everything runs down.

Did you know?

The plain fact is that nobody, but nobody, has proof of how the universe will end. Everything you read here is theory – and that goes for the scientific textbooks as well.

In this alternative scenario, the galaxies will eventually stop rushing away from one another. They'll begin to fall back, approaching closer and closer (with catastrophic results), moving through a second version of the heat death until all the matter, all the antimatter, all the time and all the space in the universe is once again packed into a single super-dense ball, just as it was in the beginning.

It may stay that way, the end of the universe in a nutshell – and an extraordinarily hot nutshell at that. Or the Big Bang may go off again, expanding the universe to repeat the process again and again in an endless cycle of endings and beginnings.

Of course all those scenarios depend on the universe doing its own expanding thing without interference. You might find it difficult to imagine *anything* could interfere with the fate of something as large as the universe, but there's an outside possibility Black Holes could.

Some scientists are convinced many (perhaps most or even all) galaxies have a Black Hole at their centre. If this is true and the Black Holes keep growing, the time may come when the gravitational field of a Black Hole is big enough to bridge the gap between galaxies. Once that happens, Black Holes will start to attract *each other,* eventually forming a single super colossal Black Hole capable of swallowing up everything in the universe.

20 How do you know the universe is expanding?

If you've ever listened to the whistle of a train, you'll know that the pitch gets higher as the train approaches, but drops in a spooky way once the train travels away from you. This shift in the sound is called the Doppler Effect and it happens with light as well. As something travels away from you, the light coming from it gets more and more red.

You won't notice this watching a train, because the effect is so tiny, but in 1929, the American astronomer Edwin Hubble did notice that the light coming from distant stars showed a marked shift towards the red end of the colour spectrum. He decided this must mean the stars he was watching were moving away from him.

But then he discovered that *whichever direction he looked,* distant stars showed a red shift. One obvious explanation was that the entire universe was expanding and that's the explanation Hubble put forward when he issued his report. Most astronomers accept this explanation today, although it's fair to say a few think there might be some other explanation for the red shift.

21 How hot was the universe when it started?

About 10,000,000,000,000°K (9,972,685,000,000°C). It cooled pretty quickly, though. After about a minute, it was down into the 1,000,000,000°K range. Which is still pretty hot, admittedly, but it's continued to cool down ever since.

it's Quiz time!

No need to look like that – I warned you in the Introduction and it's hardly my fault if you didn't read it. After every section we're going to have a really neat quiz, so you can decide at the end of this book whether you're Waste of Space or Master of the Universe. (Or possibly somewhere in between.) Here's how it works.

Answer each of the questions in Quiz Time at the end of each section. Some of the questions are tricky, but the information you need for the answer is definitely included in the section you've just finished.

There's no time limit and you're allowed to cheat as much as you can by looking things up or asking your friends (for whatever good that'll do you).

When you've tackled every question, check to see how many you got right – answers are printed upside down at the end of each Quiz Time. Make a note of your score: 1 point for every right answer.

Right at the end of the book when you've finished the final Quiz Time, add your scores together and check your rating against the table on page 127.

Got that? Course you have – it's not exactly rocket science.

Quiz 1

1 What was Einstein's first name?

2 Who discovered the red shift in distant galaxies?

3 What did he figure was causing it?

4 What do fruit flies like?

5 How far away is the nearest star?

6 What's the speed of light in kilometres per second?

7 Has it ever actually been proved that time slows down as you speed up?

8 Name either of the two physicists who discovered the background radiation of the universe.

9 What percentage of the speed of light does a muon travel?

10 What weight is a spoonful of neutron star stuff?

Answers

1. Albert 2. Edwin Hubble 3. The expansion of the universe
4 A banana 5. 4.3 light years 6. 300,000 (186,000 miles)
7. Yes 8. Arno A. Penzias or Robert W. Wilson 9. 99%
10. 1,000,000,000 tonnes

22 Why do stars twinkle?

Actually they don't. When you're standing at the observation port of the *Starship Enterprise*, every star you see will burn quite steadily without the slightest hint of twinkle. The twinkle effect only occurs on Earth and is the result of looking at the night sky through the lens of our atmosphere. In other words, it's a trick of the light.

Planets, which are visible only through reflected light, don't twinkle at all.

23 Can stars fall to Earth?

Not a chance – they're too far away. Besides, even the smallest visible star is many times larger – not to say considerably hotter – than our planet. If one came close, the Earth would burn and explode long before there was any actual contact.

The 'falling stars' you hear about aren't stars at all, but meteors. Our planet is constantly bombarded by space debris, lumps of rock that enter the atmosphere and heat up to a spectacular glow because of friction, thus taking on the appearance of a falling star.

Approximately 15 meteors burn up in the atmosphere every hour, day and night, with the numbers rising dramatically during what are known as meteor showers. Hundreds of thousands of falling stars were seen over North America on the night of November 12, 1833, for example. (November is usually a good month for observing meteors.)

Most falling stars are no bigger than a pea and burn up completely within minutes of entering the atmosphere. But a few are large enough to survive all the way to the ground. Biggest of all so far came down near Grootfontein, Namibia, in 1920. It weighed more than 60 tonnes.

24 Why do they call the Dog Star that?

What we're talking about here is the brightest star in the night sky. It was called Sothis by the Ancient Egyptians and the official astronomical name today is Sirius. It's actually two stars (one a white dwarf) orbiting around each other once every 50 years and is located about 8.6 light years away from our solar system.

The Dog Star business arises from the fact that Sirius is located in the constellation Canis Major ('the Big Dog') and bears the Latin title Alpha Canis Major, the First Star of the Big Dog constellation – hence Dog Star. The first appearance of Sirius just before sunrise in any given year is known as its heliacal rising and marked the hottest part of the year for the Ancient Romans, something we still remember when we use the expression 'dog days.'

Perhaps the weirdest thing about the Dog Star is that the Dogon, a tribe in the West African country of Mali, knew it was a binary star with a white dwarf companion long before it was discovered with the aid of modern telescopes. They claim this – and other accurate items of astronomical information – was taught to them by an alien visitor from Sirius centuries ago. Spooky.

25 What's a white dwarf?

A small person of Caucasian origin. Just kidding. In astronomy, it's one of the possibilities that's left when a small to medium-sized star reaches the end of its life.

White dwarves are white in colour (duh!), typically fairly dim and much the same size as our Earth. But the mass of a white dwarf – the amount of material it contains – is about the same as our sun, so what you have is something very dense, somewhere around a million times the density of water on average. Because they're so dim, the only ones astronomers can actually see are relatively near Earth – somewhere in the region of 300 to 900 light years away. All the same, we have a fairly good idea of what they're made of and how they are formed.

What they're made of, at the centre, is a mixture of carbon and oxygen. Surrounding that are thin layers of helium and hydrogen. How they're formed is a bit complicated. You start off with a small to medium-sized ordinary star that burns away, minding its own business, for several billion years without very much change. But as it gets older, with the bulk of its original fuel used up, changes start to occur. It goes through a couple of stages where it cools but expands, becoming a red giant.

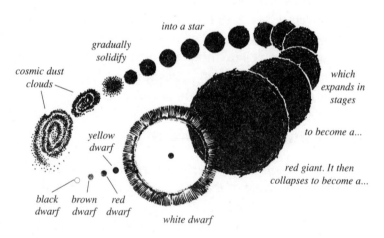

into a star

gradually solidify

cosmic dust clouds

which expands in stages

yellow dwarf

to become a...

red giant. It then collapses to become a...

black dwarf   *brown dwarf*   *red dwarf*

white dwarf

During the second of these red giant stages, the star loses its outer layers by blowing them off. With the outer layers gone, you're left with a very dense, very hot, very luminous core surrounded by a glowing shell and maybe half the size of our sun or a bit larger, depending on the original size of the star. When this cools down, it becomes a white dwarf.

SPACE QUEST

White dwarves don't have any nuclear energy left, but they still radiate a lot of heat, so they continue to glow if, in astronomy terms, only dimly. After several more billion years, even this glow fades as the star loses the last of its heat and turns into a cold husk, sometimes known as a black dwarf.

26 What's a red dwarf?

It's an old white dwarf.

There are various things that can happen to a white dwarf. One of them is that it just keeps cooling down. As it does so, it changes colour, turning yellow, red, brown and eventually black.

27 What's the most unusual star?

Outside a Black Hole (which isn't so much a star as the lack of a star), the most unusual star has to be a pulsar. To know why, you need to know about something called SETI.

SETI stands for the Search for Extra-Terrestrial Intelligence, a fancy way of saying that for some time now, astronomers have been looking for any signs that there might be intelligent life outside this planet. Various SETI programmes have come and gone, but they all have one thing in common – they use radio telescopes.

All the early telescopes worked by magnifying the light collected from distant stars. But in 1937, an American named Grote Reber built the first radio telescope, a device designed to study the natural radio emissions from stars, galaxies and other things in space.

But then it occurred to astronomer Frank Drake that *natural* emissions weren't the only things radio telescopes could study. In 1959, he set up something called Project Ozma at the National Radio Astronomy Observatory in Green Bank, West Virginia in the USA.

Ozma was a SETI project – the world's first. It used the telescope at the Green Bank Observatory to search for radio signals broadcast by any alien civilizations that might be out there.

Although the first properly funded SETI programme wasn't set up by NASA (National Aeronautics and Space Administration) until the late 1980s, word of the Ozma Project went through the astronomy community like wildfire.

Did you know?

Jocelyn Bell, the student who actually discovered the first pulsar, was never given official recognition for her find. Her boss, however, got the Nobel Prize.

Fast forward to 1967. A research student named Jocelyn Bell was at the radio telescope of the University of Cambridge when an utterly astonishing signal came through. It was the weirdest thing Bell had ever heard. Up to then, all radio signals from space had been random bursts, the sort of thing you'd expect to occur naturally. But this new signal was regular as clockwork. She called in her boss, Antony Hewish. It was the weirdest thing he'd ever heard as well.

For a while, a lot of people thought they'd cracked it.

Those regular signals just *had* to be artificial. The press had a field day and there were reports of messages from Little Green Men.

But the Bell/Hewish discovery had nothing at all to do with an advanced civilization or alien life of any sort. It was a perfectly natural object, although one unlike anything detected by astronomers before. What they'd found was the first pulsar.

28 What's a pulsar?

It's the short way of saying 'pulsating radio star' and it's anything out there that gives off very regular pulses of radio waves. A few of the pulsars astronomers have now discovered give off regular bursts of light, X-rays and gamma rays as well.

Although pulsars started out as just about the greatest mystery in astronomy, there's a lot of evidence now that they're actually fast-spinning neutron stars. Neutron stars are formed when the core of an exploding supernova falls in on itself and gets compressed to such an extent that it's little more than a tiny (20-kilometre [12-mile] diameter) ball of particles called neutrons.

On the surface of this ball, neutrons tend to decay into other types of particles like protons and electrons. These particles are thrown off into the powerful magnetic field that surrounds the star and spin right along with it. The spin makes them go faster and faster until they're close to the speed of light, at which point they start to give off radiation. What happens is this.

The magnetic poles of a pulsar are in completely different places to the physical axis of the star. So as it spins, it sends out beams of radiation at regular intervals exactly like a giant lighthouse. Every time the beam sweeps past our Earth-based telescopes, it looks as if the star is pulsing.

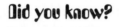

Did you know?

The great secret of the pulsar is that it doesn't pulse at all. What happens is that radiation beams from the star's magnetic poles, creating the illusion of a pulse.

More than 300 pulsars have now been discovered. The slowest of them has a four-second pulse, the fastest 1.55 milliseconds (which means it's spinning at a rate of 642 times a second). The newest pulsar we know about is in the Crab Nebula and was formed in a supernova explosion recorded by Chinese astronomers in CE 1054. Barring accidents, it will continue to radiate regularly for the next 10,000,000 years, at which point it will switch off as its magnetic field weakens.

Now you see it...

Now you don't...

Now you see it...

29 Where do the stars go in the daytime?

Nowhere. They're still up there – it's just that you can't

see them because the light from the sun swallows up everything else.

30 Can you drink the Milky Way?

Not unless you have a very big mouth. The Milky Way is the name of the galaxy of which our solar system is a part. When you look at it in the night sky, it's a river of stars so tightly packed together that it looks like a spill of milk.

Funnily enough, we now know the Milky Way isn't shaped anything like it appears from Earth. It's a spiral galaxy, 70,000 light years across, containing several billion stars and huge amounts of gas and dust. The whole thing looks a bit like a giant pinwheel.

You can't see the centre because it's hidden by all that dust, but astronomers studying radio waves, X-rays and similar radiation have come to the conclusion there's something nasty in there. All the signs are that a gigantic Black Hole, 4,000,000 times bigger than the sun, is lurking at the heart of our galaxy and may be quietly eating up the whole system.

Fortunately we live near the inner edge of one of the spiral arms, a long way from the centre, so it will be a very long time indeed before there's any chance of the Black Hole getting us.

Incidentally, our sun is in orbit around the galactic centre at a speed of 225 kilometres (140 miles) per second. Sounds fast, but at that rate it takes us 200,000,000 years to make just one complete circuit.

31 What's a star map?

It's a map showing where the known stars are in any given segment of the sky. A good star map will name the main ones.

32 Why do wizards have stars on their hats?

Some of the earliest wizards were the Magi of Persia (now Iran). Among them were the 'three wise men' of the Bible who followed the Star of Bethlehem to see Jesus born. That business of following a star gives the clue to what they were all about. The Magi, and most magicians of dawning civilizations, were astronomers who studied the heavens and astrologers who tried to foretell the future from the positions of planets and stars.

Wizards have been pictured with stars on their hats ever since.

33 How long would it take to reach the nearest star?

The nearest star to our solar system is Proxima Centauri, roughly 4.3 light years away, which makes it a trip of 39,103,109,000,000 kilometres (24,302,740,000,000 miles).

They can tell you what they like on *Star Trek,* but our fastest spaceship at the moment is the American Shuttle, which can hit speeds in excess of 40,547 km/h (25,200 mph) when pushed, but prefers to cruise at 29,000 km/h (18,000 mph).

Assuming you coaxed an average speed of 32,000 km/h (20,000 mph) out of it, you'd reach Proxima Centauri in a little over 13,871 years.

After that, you have to get back.

34 Who first studied the heavens?

The earliest known civilization – that of Sumer in the Middle East – sprang up somewhere between 4500 BCE and 4000 BCE between the Tigris and the Euphrates rivers, in what's now southern Iraq. It stretched from around Baghdad to the Persian Gulf. The area was first settled by a people called the Ubaidians, who drained the marshes for agriculture, developed trade and established industries like weaving, leatherwork, metalwork and pottery. They also made a systematic study of the stars and planets, which they seem to have linked with the activities of their gods.

The Egyptian civilization, founded around 3500 BCE also developed a sophisticated astronomy, showing a profound interest in the stars among ancient peoples generally. But neither the Egyptians nor even the Sumerians seem to have been the first students of the heavens. A carved jawbone fragment appears to have been cut to record the phases of the moon. The fragment is more than 20,000 years old.

35 Why are some star groups called after animals or people?

The human brain is very good at picking out shapes and patterns, so good, in fact, it will sometimes pick out patterns that aren't really there – which is why you can so easily imagine you see pictures in a fire.

Long ago when the people of ancient civilizations studied the night sky, certain star groupings reminded them of familiar things – a bull or an archer or a pair of scales. It was convenient to call them by these names, which have come down to us as the Signs of the Zodiac, star groupings called after people, animals and things.

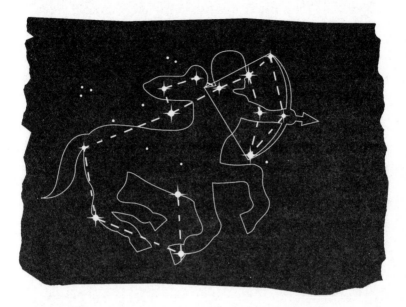

36 What makes a star blow up?

Old age, generally.

Exploding stars are sort of interesting. There are two main types and the first time an exploding star was spotted, nobody realised it was an exploding star at all. What happened was early astronomers suddenly noticed a star in a section of the sky where there had been no star before. They naturally assumed a new star had made its appearance. As 'new stars' popped up from time to time, they were labelled *'novas'* – nova being Latin for *new*.

But as equipment and techniques improved in recent times, astronomers came to realise novas weren't new stars at all. They were old stars too faint to be seen that had suddenly exploded, becoming somewhere between 1,000 and 100,000 times brighter in the process. Typically they'll stay this bright for a few days or weeks, then fade back to what they were before.

You'll find most novas occur in binary stars – that's to say systems in which two stars orbit around one another – when they get old. An old binary system will usually comprise of a red giant and a white dwarf. That's okay, except that in certain cases the red giant expands right into the gravitational field of the white dwarf.

When that happens, the strong gravity of the dwarf sucks large quantities of hydrogen out of the red giant. This material builds up on the surface of the dwarf until it triggers a vast nuclear explosion throwing out enormous quantities of surface gases. This is what makes the star suddenly brighten.

But the white dwarf isn't destroyed by the explosion. After a short time things settle down again and the dwarf goes back to shining dimly. One thing's changed, however – the explosion has blown the dwarf and the Giant further apart. All the same, if you give them enough time – maybe 100,000 years or so – they'll drift back together and the whole nova business happens again.

Did you know?

If our sun went nova – which astronomers say can't happen – it would not only vaporise you instantly, but take the whole Earth and the rest of the solar system with it.

The second type of exploding star is a supernova, which makes an ordinary nova look like a flickering candle. When a nova goes off, it's at most 100,000 times brighter than it was before. When a supernova explodes, its brightness can increase not just by thousands or even millions, but by *billions*. Like a nova, a supernova stays bright for a week or two at best, then slowly dims.

A supernova is what happens when a neutron star doesn't quite make it to the Black Hole stage. A neutron star is formed when a very large star at the end of its life starts to collapse in on itself. In some neutron stars a hard core is formed before the collapse is complete. When this happens, matter falling in as part of the ongoing collapse hits the core with such force that the resulting explosion blows off the star's outer layers.

Unlike a white dwarf nova, this more or less ruins the star. In a supernova, you can get such an enormous explosion that enough matter is thrown off to make several of our suns and enough energy generated to let the supernova outshine its entire galaxy.

One of the earliest recorded supernovas exploded in CE 1054 and was so bright it could be clearly seen in daytime. Its remains are visible to this day as the Crab Nebula.

37 What's the proper name for The Plough?

The Plough, an arrangement of seven bright stars that makes up one of the most distinctive features of the night sky in the northern hemisphere, has been (and still is) called many different names including The Wagon,

The Big Dipper, Septentriones, and Charles's Wain. For Hindus, it's the Seven Rishis. It's referred to in the Old Testament and mentioned in the Iliad.

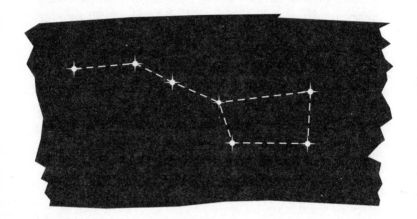

The Ancient Greeks linked The Plough with the nymph Callisto. According to Greek mythology, Callisto was turned into a bear by Zeus, the king of the gods, and placed in the heavens in that form. Consequently the Greeks named the constellation 'Arctos' which means she-bear. The Ancient Romans took up the name, although they often used their own variation Ursa, which also means she-bear.

Today, astronomers follow the old Roman custom and and use the term Ursa Major (or Great Bear) for The Plough.

38 Which is the closest star?

The third brightest star in the heavens (after Sirius and Canopus) is actually a triple system consisting of two bright stars circling each other every 80 years and orbited in turn by a red dwarf every few million years.

You can't see the red dwarf without a telescope, but it's the closest star to Earth. It's about 4.3 light years away and they call it Proxima Centauri.

39 Why does the sun shine?

Because its centre keeps exploding.

The sun's a lot bigger than you would imagine, a ball of luminous gas 1,392,00 kilometres (864,950 miles) in diameter and about 330,000 times bigger than the Earth. In fact it's so big, it makes up 99% of all the matter in the entire solar system.

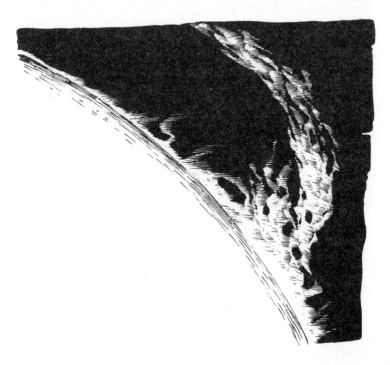

Anything this size gets compressed by its own weight. At the centre, the compressed gas is so hot that it turns into one big continuous hydrogen bomb. Five million tonnes of matter are converted into energy every second of the day. This sends the temperature of the rest soaring.

No wonder the sun shines.

40 Could our sun blow up?

No, it's too small. Only stars several times bigger than our sun have the possibility of going nova or supernova. In several billion years, as it gets old and decrepit, the sun will become a red giant and expand so much it will swallow Mercury and Venus whole. Although it won't grow enough to swallow Earth, that won't be much consolation if you're there at the time – the sun will be so close our oceans will boil off and our atmosphere will blow away.

After that it will follow the classic pattern of stars this size and eventually evolve into a dwarf, turning white, yellow, red and brown before finally dying as a black dwarf.

it's Quiz time!

Now's your chance to shine like a star. Ten more questions and exactly the same deal as before. Answer them, check your answers and keep a note of your score.

1 What colour does a red dwarf turn during the next stage of its evolution?

2 What does SETI stand for?

3 Name the first ever SETI project.

4 Name the woman who discovered the first pulsar.

5 What shape is our galaxy?

6 What Latin name do Western astronomers use for the Seven Rishis?

7 What takes up 99% of our solar system?

8 What caused the Crab Nebula?

9 What's the cruising speed of the Space Shuttle?

10 How long does it take for the sun to orbit the centre of our galaxy?

Answers

1. Brown 2. Search for Extra-Terrestrial Intelligence
3. Project Ozma 4. Jocelyn Bell 5. Spiral 6. Ursa Major
7. The sun 8. An exploding supernova
9. 29,000 km/h (18,000 mph) 10. 200,000,000 years

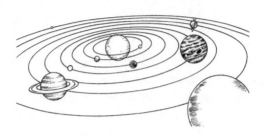

41 How long would it take to visit all the planets?

Depends what you mean by visit. Obviously if it's just a fly-past, you'll manage the job faster than if you decide to land on each and make yourself a cup of tea. But assuming you forget about landing – which you couldn't do on all the planets anyway since the high gravity giants like Jupiter and Saturn would crush you – this will give you a rough idea how long it would take.

First, you have to remember you're starting out from Earth, which is the third planet from the sun. So you have to fly sunwards in order to visit Venus and Mercury.

Mercury is approximately 77,300,000 kilometres (48,034,220 miles) from Earth at its very closest approach. If you commandeered the Shuttle and cruised at 32,000 km/h (20,000 mph) you'd reach Mercury in about 100 days. With any luck you'd fly past Venus on the way.

But to visit all the other planets, you'd have to turn round and come back again, which adds a further 100 days to the trip before you're in orbit above Earth and ready to make the outward trip.

You're heading for Pluto now, the planet most distant from the sun. That's roughly 5,744,640,000 kilometres (3,569,553,805 miles) away. Fire up the Shuttle, hope you don't get a puncture, and you should be there in 7,436 days. Add that to the 200 days you've already wasted flying to Mercury and back, and you've a grand total of 7,636 days or a bit under 21 years.

To make the sums easy, I've pretended all the other planets you want to visit en route will be nicely lined up so you can fly straight past them on your way to Pluto. But since they all orbit the sun at different speeds, this is extremely unlikely. So you'd probably have to make detours to get within spitting distance of Mars, Jupiter, Saturn, Uranus and Neptune, which will add more time, as, of course, will the journey home.

Why do you want to visit all the planets anyway?

42 Why is Mars red?

From space, our Earth shows up as a blue planet because the surface area is largely covered by water. There used to be oceans on Mars by all accounts, but there's not much surface water now, except possibly at the poles where it's locked up as ice. Today, most of Mars has a brutally cold, rubble-strewn, completely barren surface made up of reddish rock. Which is why it shows up red in the night sky.

43 Is there life on other planets?

Astronomers have long argued that since there are countless billions of stars in the universe, the chances of life evolving elsewhere than on Earth must be huge. But that's a logical deduction that falls short of proof.

Scientists also speculate that conditions on Europa, one of the moons of Jupiter, might also be favourable to life, but again there's been no definite proof.

44 Are we trying to contact people on other planets?

Oh yes, and have been since 1959. Although I suppose it's more accurate to say we've been watching out for them to contact us.

Most scientists are quite sure there's no intelligent life in the solar system beyond Earth, so the search has concentrated on messages from distant stars. The idea is that if there are any advanced civilizations out there, they'll want to talk to their neighbours and the most convenient way to do so would be to send out radio signals. So if we listen carefully with our radio telescopes, we should be able to hear them.

One drawback of this theory is that the sky's a big place and a radio telescope has to be aimed just right to pick up a signal. So you could go for years, maybe centuries, looking in the wrong place.

Despite this, we're looking and listening anyway (as we learned earlier), a process usually called the Search for Extra-Terrestrial Intelligence, or SETI.

Although the first SETI project was set up as long ago as 1959 by Frank Drake, it was strictly an unofficial affair. There wasn't much money to fund it and, not a lot of interest from the authorities, who may have found the whole concept a little sci-fi for their taste.

But by the late 1980s, the world had changed sufficiently for NASA to take an interest in the possibility of extra-terrestrial life. A massive $100 million was found to set up the first official project.

Did you know?

Frank Drake was so confident of finding evidence of extra-terrestrial life that he predicted the breakthrough would come by the year 2000. Although that deadline has come and gone, most astronomers remain optimistic.

SETI has had its ups and downs since then, including periods when American government funding was withdrawn, but seems to be doing okay just at the moment. The biggest problem of late has been the fact that SETI observatories – the main one is the massive Arecibo radio telescope in South America – have been gathering so much information they don't have the computer power to process it.

But somebody came up with an absolutely brilliant idea. There are millions of home computers all over the world that spend at least some of their time running screen savers. Why not replace the flying toasters with a screen saver that analyses SETI data?

The idea led to the establishment of the 'SETI at Home' programme, which you can take part in if you've got a computer with Internet access. You download free SETI software – there are versions available for both PC and Mac – install it into your computer and it replaces your screen saver with a special SETI analysis application. You set this running by downloading information from Arecibo and it sends your analysis back via the Internet when the batch is finished, then downloads more data.

If your computer happens to be the one that finds proof ET is out there, you become the most famous kid in the history of the known universe. You can start it all happening by pointing your browser at http://setiathome.berkeley.edu.

45 Would people on other planets look like us?

Probably not. Life evolves in relation to its environment. Conditions on other planets are likely to be quite different from those on Earth, so any life forms would be different too.

That said, I've heard it argued that the basic human shape – head, torso, arms and legs – is generally both efficient and useful, so nature may throw it up again from time to time to face the challenge of different environments.

Which means *some* humanoid aliens are a possibility.

46 What's the Face on Mars?

In 1976, two unmanned NASA space probes, *Viking I* and *Viking II*, undertook a massive photographic survey of the Martian surface.

Between them they took about 60,000 pictures.

Among these were 18 taken of the Cydonia Mensae region situated at 40.9° North latitude, 9.45° West longitude. Five of the eighteen showed a rock formation that looked like a human face.

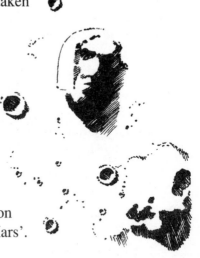

The photographs received widespread press coverage. The rock formation was dubbed the 'Face on Mars'.

47 Is there life on Mars?

In 1976, NASA scientists decided to see if they could answer that question.

On July 20 of that year, a *Viking* spacecraft in orbit around Mars launched a robot landing craft that touched down in the region of Chryse Planitia. A little over a month later, a second landing was made, this time at Utopia Planitia. Each of the landers contained a miniature laboratory designed to detect life. These little craft began to analyse atmosphere and soil samples, temperature and wind speed. Cameras took photographs of the immediate environment.

The first experiment in chemical analysis showed no trace of any organic material on the Martian surface. In the second experiment, the cameras picked up no signs of any fossils or life forms in the immediate surroundings.

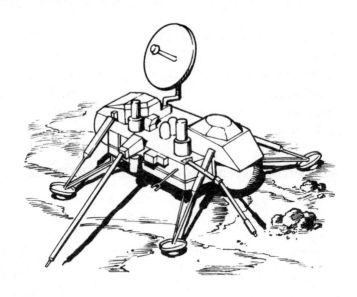

The third experiment was more complicated. It tested for photosynthesis, the process by which plants convert sunlight into sugar, and chemosynthesis, another process suggesting the presence of life. It measured gases released from soil samples exposed to damp and given nutrients. (This would show whether there were any life forms lying dormant in the soil.) Finally, it checked for radioactive gas in soil samples exposed to radioactive organic nutrients.

All three approaches produced positive results. Although some of the results would have been accepted as absolute proof of the existence of life had the experiments been carried out on Earth, the scientists in charge of the project decided no life signs were present. Today, most reports of these experiments will tell you the results were negative.

But if NASA has so far decided there's no life on Mars at the moment, they've also told us there used to be at one time. On August 6, 1996, they announced that a meteorite which crashed into the Antarctic more than 12,000 years ago contained microscopic fossil remains of living creatures. The rock originated on the surface of Mars, showing that something once lived there, perhaps millions of years ago.

48 When were the planets formed?

About the same time as the sun, according to current theory. That would make them about 4.7 billion years old. Astronomers believe the solar system started out as a cloud of gas and dust which suffered what's called gravitational collapse when a nearby supernova exploded.

One result was the formation of a dense central region with enough energy and gravity to trigger a new sun. You might say the sun 'condensed' out of the gas cloud.

Most scientists believe the other bodies in the solar system, including the Asteroid Belt, condensed as well at much the same time. There are several reasons why they believe this. One is that the region closest to the new sun would be so hot that it would stop the condensation of anything lighter than iron. Mercury, the closest planet to the sun has an unusually large, dense, iron core. At greater distances, gases condense into solids such as are found in Jupiter and the outer planets.

49 Are there any planets bigger than the Earth?

Yes. Jupiter, Saturn, Uranus and Neptune are all very much bigger than Earth. Mercury, Mars and Pluto are smaller while Venus is much the same size. The few planets now discovered outside our solar system are all bigger than Earth as well, but you'd expect that since small planets are a lot more difficult to see.

50 What's the biggest planet of them all?

Jupiter. It's actually bigger than all the other planets put together, with a volume 1,500 times greater than the Earth. It also has the strongest magnetic field of any planet, reaching well beyond Saturn, the next planet out from the sun.

Jupiter is made up mainly of hydrogen and helium, with only a very small solid core. It gives out 70% more heat than it receives from the sun so it has to have some sort of internal heat source. It also broadcasts intense bursts of radio waves and at times these become so violent they exceed the radio wave activity of the sun.

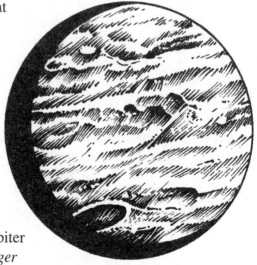

The other really big thing about Jupiter is its storms. *Voyager* and *Galileo* spacecraft photographed polar storms so massive and violent that they generated superbolts of lightning, vastly more powerful than anything we experience on Earth. (Oddly enough, Jupiter was named after the Roman king of the gods, who was believed to hurl enormous lightning bolts at anybody displeasing him.)

51 What's the red spot on Jupiter?

In 1665, the spot was first discovered by the French astronomer Gian Domenico Cassini using one of the very earliest telescopes. It probably existed long before he saw it and it has certainly existed ever since. It is oval in shape, located at latitude 23° South, and has an east-west length of about 28,000 kilometres (17,400 miles), roughly twice the diameter of the Earth. Even its north-south extent is enormous – it varies around 14,000 kilometres (8,700 miles).

Thanks to observations made by the *Galileo* and *Voyager* spacecraft, we know quite a lot about the great red spot now. It's really a high-pressure system – what we'd call an anticyclone on Earth. Here, anticyclones usually mean calm, dry, sunny weather, but on Jupiter the GRS is circled by 290 km/h (180 mph) winds and ammonia-crystal clouds.

Did you know?

Jupiter's famous red spot is actually a permanent storm that's bigger than the entire Earth.

Despite its name, it actually varies in colour from brick red to muddy brown. Nobody quite knows what causes either hue, but astronomers speculate that the massive spinning motion might suck up chemical colour elements – notably sulphur – from inside the planet. (Jupiter is what's known as a gas giant and lacks all but a tiny solid core, so this is entirely possible.)

While the great red spot wanders in longitude, it maintains its latitudinal position quite firmly and nobody is quite sure why or how. Certainly it's not fixed to anything (because there's nothing in the neighbourhood it *could* be fixed to) yet with all the turbulence around it, it's difficult to see how it could be self-sustaining… except that clearly it is!

52 How high could I jump on Jupiter?

You couldn't jump at all. The massive gravity would crush you like a gnat.

53 What's the smallest planet then?

Pluto.

Pluto is usually referred to as the outermost planet of the solar system, although it has such a peculiar orbit there are times when it moves closer to the sun than Neptune. It's a titchy little planet with lots of its surface area covered in methane ice. With a diameter of 2,300 kilometres (1,430 miles) it's only about two thirds the size of our moon.

The next smallest planet is Mercury, but with a

diameter of 4,870 kilometres (3,050 miles) that's more than twice as big as Pluto.

54 How hot is it on Mercury?

Depends on the time of day.

Mercury is the planet in our solar system that's closest to the sun – just about 58,000,000 kilometres (35,960,000 miles) away on average. It's small – only 4,870 km (3,050 miles) in diameter – and it has a very elliptical, stretched-out, orbit.

Mercury whizzes round the sun at 48 kilometres (29.8 miles) a second so its year is only 88 Earth-days long. (Which is why it's called Mercury, incidentally. In Ancient Rome, Mercury was the messenger of the gods and had wings on his feet for an extra burst of speed.) But it turns very slowly on its axis, taking 59 Earth-days to complete a single revolution.

Now this is a bit tricky to visualise. On Earth, the period of the planet's revolution – 24 hours – is the same as a single day, measured as the time between one sunrise and the next. But on Mercury, the fact that it's whizzing round the sun so fast has to be taken into consideration, so the time between each sunrise is fully 176 Earth-days.

That means for an average of 88 Earth-days, one half of Mercury is baking in the sunshine, while the other half, the night side, is shivering in the dark. Because the planet is so small, its gravity is too weak to hold onto much of an atmosphere. There's some hydrogen, oxygen, carbon dioxide, krypton, argon and xenon up there, but not enough to write home about. With next to no atmosphere, there's nothing to keep in the heat.

Put all these various things together and you might guess there would be a very great variation in the surface temperatures of Mercury. And you'd be right. It gets as hot as 402°C when the sun comes out, but drops to −173°C after dark.

55 What's the weather like on Venus?

Dreadful.

Although Venus is named after the Ancient Roman goddess of love and beauty, its surface conditions are about as hostile and ugly as they could possibly get. Because Venus is almost exactly the same size as the Earth and is the brightest object in the night sky after the moon, astronomers in the old days used to speculate about the possibility of water there, with plant growth and even intelligent life.

But unmanned space probes soon put paid to that nonsense.

We now know that Venus has an atmosphere consisting of 96% carbon dioxide and about 3.5% nitrogen, with tiny amounts of carbon monoxide, sulphur dioxide, helium, water vapour and argon making up the rest. That carbon dioxide content may point to a runaway 'greenhouse effect' – the sort of thing that worries scientists about our own global warming just now – at some time in the past. But however it came about, the planet has a surface temperature of 460°C, the highest of any planet in the solar system, including Mercury which is a lot nearer the sun.

Did you know?

The astronomer Carl Sagan once compared surface conditions on Venus to the medieval vision of Hell, and calculated that to survive there you would need to be squat, immensely strong, with a leathery skin and possibly stubby bat wings to navigate the atmosphere ... just like the old idea of devils.

About 45 km (28 miles) above the surface, there's an unbroken layer of cloud some 24 km (15 miles) thick extending across the planet. The cloud is made almost entirely of concentrated sulphuric acid. Although Venus rotates on its axis very slowly – a day is 243 Earth-days long – astronomers have observed features in the upper atmosphere that travelled round the entire planet in only 96 hours, which suggests high wind speeds.

If you travelled to Venus, you'd find most of the planet consisted of gently rolling plains strewn with flat slabs of basalt rock and broken up by the occasional active volcano. So far as weather is concerned, you would take your morning stroll in perpetual gloom, baking in temperatures hot enough to melt lead and lashed by vicious acid rain driven by hurricane winds.

Bring your umbrella.

56 Will we be invaded by aliens from another planet?

Good question, but the answer's sort of complicated.

First, what do you mean by aliens? If it's just life forms from Outer Space, then there are serious scientists who'll tell you it's already happened. Some astronomers, like the late Fred Hoyle, believe that disease-causing microbes sometimes land on Earth, carried by meteorites. This, they say, is what causes sudden, unexpected epidemics like the influenza that followed World War One or the Black Death that wiped out much of Europe in the fourteenth century.

But when most people ask about alien invasions, they're usually thinking of intelligent life in spaceships armed with phasers, photon torpedoes and all that sort of stuff. How likely is an invasion of this sort?

To answer that question, you have to ask yourself where the invasion will come from. There may have been life on Mars at one time and there may still be life elsewhere in our solar system (on Europa for example, one of the moons of Jupiter). But most scientists are happy that if there was intelligent life advanced enough to build spaceships, we'd have found it by now. So invasion by aliens within our solar system isn't really on the cards.

The next possibility is an invasion from Outer Space, aliens from a distant star or galaxy. Although you'll find galaxy class starships crawling over almost every sci-fi movie in the past ten years, many scientists aren't at all sure inter-stellar travel is actually possible. They argue that the distances between the stars are just too great.

The nearest planet theoretically capable of supporting life outside our solar system orbits 70 Virginis, which is 50 light years away.

Did you know?

A radio play based on H.G.Wells' novel *The War of the Worlds* (which described an invasion of Earth by Martians) once caused widespread panic in America. People thought the fictional news broadcasts that started the play were the real thing.

In 1961, a Nobel prize-winning physicist named Edward Purcell worked out the energy requirements of rockets that could travel at a worthwhile fraction of the speed of light. The figure was so enormous he concluded no civilization, however advanced, could possibly take to inter-stellar travel. He said the idea belonged on the back of cereal boxes.

Even if you could somehow accelerate your rocket to the speed of light (which Einstein's calculations show is quite impossible) 100 plus years is an awfully long time to chug through space, invade a planet and bring back your spoils of war. There are even some scientists who argue that if you had a civilization technically advanced enough to cross the galaxy, it would be morally advanced enough not to invade lesser species.

All this sounds very plausible, but there are flaws in the arguments. A really long-lived race of aliens might find it worthwhile to spend centuries crossing space. There has been no sign on this planet that technical advances are accompanied by advanced morality. Even Einstein's discovery that you can't *accelerate* a solid body beyond the speed of light still leaves you room (if you were technically advanced enough) to build a spaceship out of material that was *already* travelling faster than light.

Our ideas of what might be possible are constantly changing. If Black Holes can distort space and time (which they can) a really advanced technology might find artificial ways of doing the same, thus shortening the distance to other star systems. In other words, while nobody thinks an alien invasion is actually likely, it can't *quite* be ruled out altogether.

57 What are Saturn's rings made of?

Ice mainly.

In 1610, Galileo became the first astronomer to discover Saturn had *something* attached to it, but through his primitive telescope it looked like handles. But 49 years later, Christiaan Huygens turned a more powerful instrument in the planet's direction and saw the handles were actually a ring system. He thought it had to be very thick and completely solid.

Today we know Huygens was just as wrong about the rings as Galileo. On average they're just a few hundred metres thick (so thin they can't be seen at all edge on) and are made up of billions of bits ranging in size from a grain of dust to asteroid-like bodies several kilometres across. Most of these bits seem to be coated in ice, which, when you put it all together, makes up the bulk of the ring material.

58 Which is our nearest planet?

Venus. Because of our orbit and its orbit, the actual distance varies, but it gets as close as 38,200,000 kilometres (23,736,379 miles) from time to time.

The next closest is Mars, which swings by at 56,000,000 kilometres (34,796,786 miles) at its nearest approach.

All the same, NASA is planning a manned flight to Mars as its next big project.

59 Are there really canals on Mars?

No. The canal business was the result of a mistranslation.

While he was looking at Mars in 1877 through the telescope at the Brera Observatory in Milan, an Italian astronomer named Giovanni Virginio Schiaparelli noticed a series of straight lines crossing the planetary surface. They seemed to extend hundreds, even thousands, of kilometres.

When Schiaparelli published his findings, he said the lines were most likely channels on the Martian surface. But once his papers were translated into English, the word for channels ('canali') was mistaken for 'canals'.

This led to the idea that the 'canals' might have been dug by intelligent beings. An American astronomer, Percival Lowell, took up the ball and ran with it. In the 1890s, he theorized that intelligent inhabitants of Mars had constructed a planet-wide irrigation system, tapping water from the polar ice caps which melted annually.

Lowell's ideas failed to stand the test of time. When the US spacecraft *Mariner IV* made a close approach to Mars in July 1965, the pictures it sent back showed no artificial canals. Although there really are immense straight-line formations on the planet, the photographs show they are mountains, chains of craters, contour boundaries, fault lines or ridges.

60 What stops the planets falling into the sun?

If you tie a weight (securely!) to a piece of string and

whirl it around your head, you've more or less got the answer. You're the sun, the string is gravity and the weight is a planet. So long as the weight keeps moving, it won't fall down.

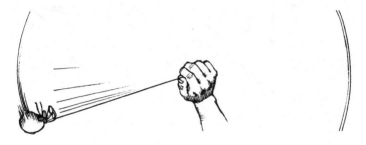

Planetary orbits are a lot more complicated than the string and weight business, but the principle's much the same. Instead of falling *into* the sun, they keep falling *round* it.

61 Who owns Mars?

Nobody, unless there turn out to be Martians, in which case *they* do.

But the whole question of ownership of things in space is messy and likely to get a lot more so. There are, for example, companies which claim to be able to sell you bits of land on the moon. Pay your money and you get a nice certificate and a map reference.

Schemes of this sort are based on the idea that you can legally lay claim to parcels of land that nobody else owns, on a first-come, first-served basis. The ownership of much of America was established this way – you literally fenced off a piece of land, a process called 'staking your claim', and the government recognised that you owned it legally once you completed a registration process.

Whether you can do something of this sort with whole planets is something that has yet to be tested in the courts. Nobody's in any hurry to do so just yet, but there are valuable mineral resources in the solar system and once it becomes practical to mine them, the question of ownership will have to be sorted, probably by international treaty.

And even this won't be the end of the story if we ever come across alien species who have their own ideas on the matter …

62 Who gave the planets their names?

The planets you can see with the naked eye all got their names in ancient times and were called after gods. (Indeed, there was a time when people believed the planets actually *were* the gods, or at least their bright bodies.) Thus you have Mercury, the messenger of the gods; Venus, the goddess of love; Mars, the god of war; Jupiter, the king of the gods and Saturn, the god of agriculture.

When a new planet was discovered in 1781, there was an attempt to call it after the astronomer who found it, Sir William Herschel, but the name didn't stick and astronomers quickly returned to the tradition of calling planets after gods. Thereafter planet Herschel became Uranus, the Greek god who personified heaven.

When Neptune was discovered in 1846, nobody thought for a minute of calling it after J. G. Galle – it was named after the Roman sea god. Same went for

Pluto, discovered in 1930 and promptly named after the mythic god of the Underworld.

63 Do all planets spin?

All the ones we know about. So apparently do stars.

it's Quiz time!

③

Time for your third quiz now. You know the form: answer the questions, check your answers and make a note of your score.

1   Name the one place in the solar system (other than Earth) where scientists think conditions might favour life.

2   What region of Mars has the rock formation that looks like a human face?

3   Where did the meteorite land that NASA scientists believe contains microscopic fossils of ancient life on Mars?

4   Name a spacecraft that has photographed Jupiter.

5   What did astronomer Gian Domenico Cassini discover in 1665?

6   Which is the second smallest planet in the solar system?

7   What are clouds made from on Venus?

8   Who discovered the rings of Saturn?

9   Who started the story of canals on Mars?

10 Which planet was originally called 'Herschel'?

64 How big is the moon?

It's a bit less than a third of the size of the Earth, with a diameter of approximately 3,476 kilometres (2,160 miles). It also weighs less, volume for volume, than our planet. A cubic centimetre of moon stuff weighs on average 3.34 grams, while the same amount of Earth stuff turns the scales at 5.52 grams.

Unlike the sun, the moon doesn't produce its own light – it acts like a giant mirror. But while the full moon looks bright on a clear night, the amount of sunlight it actually reflects is extremely tiny – just 0.073% of light received.

This is a bit odd, but not nearly so odd as the fact that the moon takes the same time to orbit the Earth as it does to spin once on its own axis. This is an astonishing coincidence and one that means the moon always keeps the same face towards Earth. Or nearly the same face. There are slight variations in the moon's orbit that mean tiny changes to the face of the moon we see from Earth. But the point is we have never, ever seen the back of the moon from the surface of our planet and never, ever will.

That's not to say we don't know what the far side looks like, of course. It was first photographed by a Soviet space probe in 1959 and turned out to be much the same in appearance as the near side.

65 Where did the moon come from?

They've been asking that since the Renaissance – about 500 years ago.

Any theory of where the moon came from has to explain how it behaves in relation to the Earth, including the fact that it is gradually moving farther away and its rate of spin is slowing.

Over the past centuries, astronomers put forward three main ideas. One was that the Earth and the moon were formed together at the birth of the solar system millions of years ago. The dust cloud that gradually solidified into the planets produced the moon at the same time. Thus Earth and moon have always been paired, right from the very beginning. It's a nice idea, but it doesn't really explain the way the moon moves.

Another idea was that when the Earth was little more than a huge blob of molten matter in the early years of the solar system, it rotated so quickly that it threw off an enormous mass of material which spun off into space, formed itself into a globe and became the moon. Unfortunately this one didn't stand up either. Once they did their sums, the scientists discovered it just wasn't possible for the Earth to throw off anything that would turn into the moon as we know it.

Did you know?

A German writer named Hans Horbiger theorized that our moon was just one of several moons, all of which had fallen to Earth causing unimaginable devastation. His ideas were taken very seriously by leaders of the Nazi Party in the 1930s, some of whom believed the present moon would fall as well.

The third idea was that the moon was captured. What you had was a moon originally formed somewhere else in the solar system (or just possibly outside it). At some time in the distant past, it strayed too close to Earth and was caught by our planet's gravity. It went into orbit and has stayed there ever since.

This idea has always been the most popular of the three. It explained a lot of things about the Earth-moon system and while the circumstances needed to catch the moon and spin it into orbit were very peculiar, they weren't quite impossible.

Once we started sending space probes to the moon, scientists began learning a lot more about it and the new knowledge had its influence on the various theories. For example, the fact that the moon is now known to be less dense than the Earth suggests they couldn't have been formed together at the beginning of the solar system.

What scientists now believe happened is this. Some time more than four billion years ago, the Earth was struck a glancing blow by something the size of Mars.

A vast cloud of fragments was thrown off to form a ring around the Earth, a little like the rings of Saturn, but very, very hot. Over millions of years, the material of this ring gradually came together to form the moon.

While we have no absolute proof that this really did happen, computer models show it certainly could have happened once you assume certain fairly likely starting circumstances. Once the moon started to form, it would quickly have swept up the rest of the ring debris, leaving the system as we see it today.

66 Could I breathe on the moon?

Not without help. It doesn't have any air.

But it does have an atmosphere of sorts. A day on the moon is two (Earth) weeks long. During this time atoms are thrown off the moon's surface and ionized into a thin gas by the solar wind. On the nightside, temperatures drop enough to trap any gases capable of condensation.

The bottom line of all this is that if you look really, really hard you'll find neon, hydrogen, helium and argon on the moon, but no oxygen. You can understand the breathing problems.

67 Is there really a man in the moon?

There used to be.

In 1968, America's Apollo project sent three astronauts William Anders, Frank Borman and James Lovell into orbit around the moon. On July 20 the following year, *Apollo 11* astronaut Neil Armstrong

became the first man on the moon, closely followed by his colleague Buzz Aldrin.

They didn't stay, of course, so until somebody goes back, the only man in the Moon is the series of natural features on its surface that combine to look like a face when seen from Earth.

68 Why is it so hard to get to the moon?

Well, it's quite a long way away for one thing.

The moon is what's known as a satellite, which means it revolves around our planet. Although it's by far the nearest astronomical body, it's still about 384,400 kilometres (239,900 miles) away.

To reach somewhere like that, you have to escape from the Earth's gravity. We've only been able to do that since 1957 when the Russians launched *Sputnik*, the first piece of equipment to go into orbit around our planet.

The Russians used a rocket to get *Sputnik* up there, as did the Americans when they finally got their astronauts to the moon in 1969. Rocket technology is very tricky – what you're really doing is sitting on top of a controlled explosion – and can go wrong at the drop

of a hat. They don't talk about it much, but the Americans had a lot of failures before Neil Armstrong went for his lunar stroll.

Did you know?

Science fiction author H. G. Wells suggested we might reach the moon by manufacturing a material that blocked out gravity. (He called it cavourite.*) Such a material was widely believed to be impossible until 2002, when newspapers reported scientific claims that the first steps had been taken to develop it.*

Even when you make a big enough rocket and get it working safely, you have to guide it to the moon. When you look up at the sky at full moon on a clear night, that doesn't seem so hard. But you have to remember you're standing on one fast-moving sphere aiming at another fast-moving sphere. To get from one to the other, your computers have to make an awful lot of calculations and corrections.

Making a rocket trip is a very tough undertaking. So tough it requires months of rigorous training and a body that doesn't have any major defects to begin with. Trying to get a couch potato like me off the planet would probably kill me.

On top of this, reaching the moon involves a period of zero gravity for your astronauts, which takes some getting used to and is very bad for them if prolonged – you lose muscle mass and physical fitness in zero gravity at a rate you wouldn't believe.

Finally there's the danger of an accident. Your guidance system could go wrong and send you off into the depths of space. Your living quarters could get punctured by a meteorite. Your fuel tank could catch fire and explode.

Frankly, when you start to think how hard it is to get to the moon, it's a miracle we ever managed it at all.

69 What's the moon made of?

Okay, we'll forget all the green-cheese jokes and take the question seriously. The moon looks as if it might be an old, worn-out planet. It has a crust and a mantle like our Earth and it may just have a small, dense, metal core, although scientists aren't sure about that. There's a mystery about the crust as well, which is thicker on the far side of the moon than on the side that faces Earth, and we have no idea why.

Most of the lunar surface is composed of rock. On the

flat maria (the name given to flat surface features once believed, incorrectly, to be seas), most of the rocks are basalt with a high iron and/or titanium content. In the highlands you get mainly anorthosite rocks containing aluminium, calcium and silicon.

A lot of the rock in both areas is so broken up you're really talking about rubble. While we haven't collected enough bedrock samples yet to be absolutely sure what's underneath, the chances are it's more of the same, except less broken.

There's soil on the moon, broken down from rock as on Earth, but in a wholly different way. On Earth, soil gradually forms due to rocks weathering – they're slowly worn down by the action of wind and rain. Without water or much of an atmosphere, the moon doesn't have either. So moon soils are the result of rock bombardment by tiny meteorites and radiation.

As well as the basic materials from the rocks that formed them, lunar soils contain small amounts of meteoritic iron and even smaller amounts of carbon which probably come from comets.

70 Are there any other moons?

Loads of them. Mars has two, Jupiter has at least 16, Uranus 15, Saturn 19 or 20 – we're not sure which. But our familiar moon is the only moon circling Earth.

71 Why can't birds fly to the moon?

A science fiction writer wrote a story about how men visited the moon in a carriage drawn by a flock of geese.

Fun thought, but it couldn't have happened.

Birds fly by flapping their wings, which push down on the air and keep them aloft in much the same way as pushing down with our feet keeps us afloat in water when we doggy paddle.

This system is great for flying generally, but only works in air. The higher you fly from the Earth's surface, the thinner the air becomes – which is why commercial aircraft are pressurised: there's not enough air for you to breathe outside. Eventually it runs out altogether, long before you ever get near the moon.

But even if you had air all the way to the moon, birds still couldn't fly there. You have to reach an exceptionally high speed to break the grip of Earth's gravity – this is called 'escape velocity' – and there's not a bird on the planet that could come anywhere close.

72 Is there anybody buried on the moon?

Not exactly buried, but after the great American astronomer Eugene (Gene) Shoemaker died in 1997, arrangements were made to have his ashes flown to the moon and placed on the surface by the Lunar Prospector. The vacuum-sealed capsule was wrapped around with a piece of brass foil on which was inscribed the following quotation from William Shakespeare:

And, when he shall die,
Take him and cut him out in little stars,
And he will make the face of heaven so fine
That all the world will be in love with night,
And pay no worship to the garish sun.

73   Could you hear somebody shouting on the moon?

Nope. You need an atmosphere to carry sound. Although the moon does have an atmosphere, it's so thin it makes for a better vacuum than you could create in most laboratories on Earth.

74   Who discovered the moons of Mars?

Officially the credit goes to the American astronomer Asaph Hall who announced in 1877 that Mars had two satellites.

Both are small, irregular in shape and reflect less than half as much light as our own moon. The inner satellite of the two orbits Mars once every 7.65 (Earth) hours at a distance of 9,378 kilometres (5,814 miles) and is ever so slowly being drawn closer to the planet so that in a billion years or so it will crash and disintegrate. The outer satellite circles the planet every 30.3 hours at a distance of 23,459 kilometres (14,545 miles).

But there's a peculiar question mark over whether Hall really was the first to discover the moons of Mars. In 1726, Dean Jonathan Swift published his famous *Gulliver's Travels*, a fantasy that contained this text:

> *They [the Laputans] have ... discovered two ...*
> *Satellites, which revolve about Mars; whereof the*
> *innermost is distant from the Center of the primary*
> *Planet exactly three of his Diameters, and the*
> *outermost five; the former revolves in the space of*
> *ten Hours, and the latter in Twenty-one and an Half;*

*so that the Squares of their periodical Times, are
very near in the same Proportion with the Cubes of
their Distance from the Center of Mars; which
evidently shews them to be governed by the same
Law of Gravitation, that influences the other
heavenly Bodies.*

A story has it that when Hall heard of Swift's
prediction, he was so overawed that he named the
satellites Phobos and Deimos – 'Fear' and 'Terror.'

Curiously, Dean Swift was not the only one to realize
Mars had two moons long before their official discovery.
The satellites are mentioned in the works of Ancient
writers Homer and Virgil. French author, Voltaire, wrote
about them in his *Micromegas,* published in 1752.
Twenty years later, they turned up again in the work of
another French writer, the Marquis de Sade.

75 Why haven't people gone to live on the moon?

The money ran out and the Cold War stopped.

After 1945, the world was split between two fiercely
competitive superpowers, the United States and the
Soviet Union. When the Soviets launched the world's
first unmanned satellite, *Sputnik 1*, in October 1957, the
shock of it drove the Americans to get into a space race.

In 1961, President John F. Kennedy announced the
Apollo Moon Program with the promise to land men on
the Moon by 1970. (They managed it with a year to
spare.) Throughout the sixties, people got very gung-ho
about space travel and there was talk of colonising the

moon by building domes for people to live in.

Scientists are pretty sure you could create living space on the moon, but, like space flight itself, this sort of project is hideously expensive. At the height of the Cold War – which is what the competition between America and the Soviet Union was called – you could justify massive spending to show you could do better than the other fellow. But towards the end of the 1980s, the Cold War thawed a lot and by 1991, the Soviet Union had collapsed completely, so showing off in space no longer seemed all that important.

As a result, far less money was pumped into the American space programme as a whole. Expensive luxuries like sending a few families to live on the moon were quietly pushed aside.

All the same, fashions change and with the advent of the new millennium, there's a growing feeling abroad that maybe we should think of pushing into space again. Certainly NASA has been working hard to drum up interest in a manned Mars landing, so the possibility of people under domes on the moon at some stage in the future shouldn't be ruled out completely.

it's **Quiz** time! (4)

Let's find out how much you know about the moon now. Answer the questions, check your answers and keep your score.

1 How long (in Earth time) is a day on the moon?

2 Who was the second man to walk on the moon?

3 What was the name of the moon programme announced by President Kennedy in 1961?

4 Is there any soil on the moon?

5 What was the name of the first artificial satellite to orbit the Earth?

6 How far away is the moon?

7 How many moons has Mars?

8 Name the astronomer who discovered them?

9 What year was the first manned moon landing?

10 How many moons has Uranus?

76 What's inside the world?

Right at the middle you have a core of solid iron. This is surrounded by an outer core of molten iron which accounts for about half the size of the entire planet. Outside this you have a rocky mantle and a crust, separated by something called the Mohorovicic discontinuity.

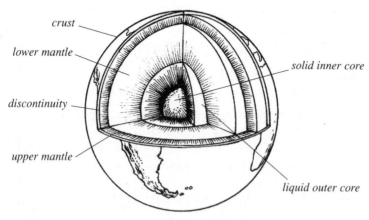

crust

lower mantle

discontinuity

upper mantle

solid inner core

liquid outer core

The Mohorovicic discontinuity is a mysterious boundary between mantle and crust discovered in 1909 by a Croatian scientist named Andrija Mohorovicic, who noticed earthquake waves moved more quickly through this area than they do elsewhere. What this says about the boundary is still anybody's guess, but it does mean there's an area of something separating the mantle from the crust that's different in composition from either.

The largest layer of crust lies under the ocean and is made mainly from basalt. The rest is continental and mainly granite.

77　What keeps people in Australia from falling off the Earth?

Gravity.

The Earth's gravitational field draws things towards its centre. Since the Earth is ball-shaped (more or less) it doesn't matter where you stand on its surface, you're still drawn the same way. So whether you're in Australia or Aberdeen, you can't fall off.

78　How old is our planet?

Near as we can tell, it's 4,600,000,000 years old.

79　What's the fastest thing in the world?

Light. At 300,000 kilometres (186,000 miles) per second, it's the fastest thing in the universe.

Next to that, you have the stuff whizzing around in cyclotrons, synchrotrons, and synchrocyclotrons – large machines used by physicists for accelerating things like electrons and protons up to very high speeds to see what will happen to them.

But if you're thinking of transport, the fastest thing in the world has to be a rocket engine. So far we haven't found any propulsion system to beat it. Modern rockets carry their own fuel and oxidizer so they don't need air to burn and consequently can travel both in space and in the atmosphere.

The world's biggest space rocket, the US *Saturn V*, is a three-stager weighing 3000 tonnes when it's fuelled up and ready to go. The first stage burns kerosene while the second and third burn liquid hydrogen. It's capable of travelling faster than 40,547 km/h (25,200 mph), which allows it to leave the surface of the Earth and head into space.

The fastest mammal in the world is the cheetah, a hunting cat that can hit speeds of 110 kilometres (70 miles) per hour so it could run you down from a standing start even if you were on your bike.

80 How do we know the Earth is round?

Easy – we look at the photographs. There are lots of them now, taken from orbiting satellites, moon shots and so on. All of them show Earth looking blue and beautiful and round.

Before we managed to get cameras off the planet, the shape of the Earth had to be worked out from things like the curvature of the horizon and the fact that a ship disappears from sight bit by bit as it sails out to sea.

Back in the Middle Ages, most people believed the Earth was flat and long-distance sailors risked falling over the edge. But in 1519, the Portuguese navigator

Ferdinand Magellan set out on a voyage that blew the notion out of the water. Although Magellan himself was killed on Mactan Island in 1521, his ships continued on to circle the globe.

81 Why is the sky blue?

It's only blue in the daytime, as you may have noticed. The colour results from the way our atmosphere filters light. If you looked up from the moon – which has no atmosphere worth talking about – the sky would be black, just like the night sky on Earth.

82 Which was the first animal in space?

A dog called Laika, sent into orbit round the Earth in 1957 by the Soviet Union as part of their Sputnik satellite programme.

83 Who was the first person?

Yury Alekseyevich Gagarin, a 27-year-old Russian, born the son of a carpenter on a collective farm near Gzhatsk.

Yury graduated from the Soviet Air Force cadet school in 1957 and just four years later, on April 12, 1961, he was strapped into the 4.75 tonne *Vostok 1* spacecraft and blasted 301 kilometres (187 miles) into Earth orbit at just after 9 a.m. He circled the planet once in 1 hour 29 minutes before landing again at 10.55 a.m.

His two-hour space flight – the very first ever – earned him the titles Hero of the Soviet Union and Pilot Cosmonaut of the Soviet Union. He was awarded the Order of Lenin and became within days the most famous person in the world. Streets were named after him and his statue erected in towns and cities across his native Russia.

Yury Gagarin

But he never went into space again and was killed in 1968 when his two-seater jet aircraft crashed on a routine training flight.

84 Could a comet blow up the world?

Back in the nineteenth century, the French astronomer Édouard Roche calculated how close one large astronomical body can approach another before the smaller of the two is torn apart by tidal forces. It turned out to be 2.5 times the radius of the larger body. Modern astronomers think that the rings of Saturn (which lie inside that planet's Roche Limit) may be the remains of a moon torn apart in this way.

For something to blow up our world, it would have to be bigger than the Earth and approach us closer than 2.5 times its own radius. No visiting comet on record is anything like the required size, although one of the supercomets recently discovered in Deep Space might do the trick if it ever entered our solar system.

But while the comets we know about wouldn't blow our planet to smithereens, many of them would do very serious damage if they crashed into the Earth. A few might be big enough to wipe out civilization and cause the sort of extinction scientists now believe wiped out the dinosaurs.

85 Could an asteroid wipe out civilization?

Mmmm, well, actually yes – and asteroids worry astronomers a lot more than comets.

The problem is asteroids aren't confined to the Asteroid Belt between Mars and Jupiter. Some of them pass sunside of Mars and so are classified as 'near-Earth' asteroids. But for a long time that just meant they were nearer to our planet than Mars was – they were still far too far away to be of any concern.

Then in 1932, a German astronomer named Karl Wilhelm Reinmuth found a group of asteroids that actually crossed Earth's orbit. That was a real shock to everybody and astronomy was in for a nerve-wracking time because, having found them, Reinmuth promptly lost them again. Asteroids don't reflect light well and so are very, very difficult to track.

While quite a few of his astronomer colleagues searched hard for Reinmuth's missing asteroids, nobody found them for more than 40 years. We were in the nasty position of knowing there were large rocks out there capable of crashing into Earth, but not having enough information to calculate whether or not they would.

In 1976, American astronomer Eleanor F. Helin found some more of them. By 1978, Reinmuth's original group had been rediscovered. This made astronomers wonder if there might be even more asteroids crossing the orbit of our planet and they set up a special study. Within two years, they'd discovered a total of 25. During the 1980s, the total had jumped to more than 100. Another 54 were added in the early 1990s.

Astronomers are now convinced there are more than 2,000 really big asteroids – more than three-quarters of a kilometre (about half a mile) in diameter, that is – regularly crossing our planet's orbit. In 1991, an asteroid came so close to the Earth it was less than half the distance of the Moon. That one was smaller than three-quarters of a kilometre in diameter, but still big enough to wipe out London had it hit.

Did you know?

In August 2002, an asteroid nearly three-quarters of a kilometre wide came closer to our planet than the moon.

In 1996, two American astronomers, Tim Spahr and Carl Hergenrother, spotted something a whole lot bigger approaching Earth. Except for our moon, this asteroid was the largest object to come this close to our planet since modern astronomical record-keeping began in 1833. It looked to be on a collision course, but seven hours from impact, it swung away again – the only reason you are reading these words now.

Despite what they show you in the movies, our only defence against space rocks is our atmosphere, which burns up most of the 40 tonnes of junk that impacts on us every year. But occasionally, bits of rock are too big to burn up completely. If a piece the size of a cricket ball gets through and strikes the planet with enough speed, it will release much the same amount of energy as the atom bomb that destroyed Hiroshima. In 1931, something just a little bigger wiped out 1,295 square kilometres (500 square miles) of rainforest in Brazil.

In 1996, NASA announced evidence of not one but a whole series of impacts by 1.6 kilometre-sized (1 mile) objects in prehistoric Africa. A single 1.6 kilometre-sized (1 mile) object travelling at 37 miles a second will release energy on impact equivalent to 300,000,000,000 tonnes of high explosive.

That's not *quite* enough to wipe out civilization,

although it would obviously make a huge mess of the country in which it lands. But something just three times larger – and there are several near-Earth asteroids of this size – would trigger massive earthquakes and tidal waves as it scattered superheated debris over thousands of kilometres.

The debris would cause widespread fires. The fires would produce smoke. The smoke would combine with the millions of tonnes of atmospheric dust thrown up by the original impact to block out the sun. Without sunshine, plants would die. Without plants, animals would have nothing to eat. In a few months, humanity would starve.

Did you know?

A really big asteroid impact wouldn't just wipe out civilization, it would cause the extinction of the entire human race.

The only good news is that a few governments are starting to take the asteroid threat seriously and are funding projects designed to deal with the problem. Meanwhile scientists have already come up with some ideas, like attaching rocket motors to the surface of the asteroid to divert it away from Earth or building an orbiting mirror that would concentrate the sun's rays like a laser and destroy an approaching asteroid completely.

We have the technology to carry through both these ideas, although nobody pretends they would be easy. But the real problem is spotting the approaching asteroid.

The big fear is that by the time astronomers discover an asteroid on a collision course with Earth, it may be too late to do anything about it.

86 What's an asteroid?

It's a very, very small planet and there are more than 7,000 of them in orbit between Mars and Jupiter. How they were first discovered is sort of interesting.

Back in 1766, a German astronomer called Johann Daniel Titus announced he'd worked out a new way of calculating the average distance of each planet from the sun. Nobody paid much attention, but another astronomer, Johann Bode, made such a fuss about the formula in 1772 that it actually came to be named after him – Bode's Law.

The exact calculation of Bode's Law is fairly complicated, but as a rule of thumb you can take it that the Law states each planet orbits the sun at about twice the distance of the previous one. At the time it was first announced, only six planets were known and it worked for five of them. Mercury, Venus, Earth, Mars and Saturn all obeyed the law, but for some reason Jupiter didn't.

When William Herschel discovered Uranus in 1781, it obeyed the law as well. Astronomers began to wonder if it had really failed in the case of Jupiter, or whether there was another new planet waiting to be discovered where Bode's Law predicted between Mars and Jupiter. They started a serious search and on New Year's Day, 1801, an Italian named Guiseppe Piazzi found what everybody was looking for. Right where Bode's Law predicted it should be, he discovered the strangest planet of the solar system. It had a most peculiar orbit and with a diameter of just 1,030 kilometres (640 miles) it was smaller than most of the known moons.

Small or not, it was a planet. It was given the name Ceres.

Just over a year later, another one turned up and was eventually given the name Pallas. It was even smaller than Ceres, but it was orbiting the sun just as any respectable planet should. The man who found it, a German astronomer named Heinrich Olbers, predicted many more similar objects would soon be found, varying in brightness and with orbits just as peculiar as Ceres and Pallas.

He was absolutely right. It quickly turned out there was an absolutely massive asteroid belt lying between the orbits of Mars and Jupiter.

Of the thousands of rocks that make up this belt, only about 250 of them have a diameter of more than 100 kilometres (62 miles) and of these only 30 have a diameter of more than 200 kilometres (124 miles). The rest vary in size downwards to the sort of boulders you might dig up in your back garden. Most meteorites recovered on Earth are now believed to be bits of asteroids, except for a very few that have been traced to the moon or Mars – and even these may have been 'splashed off' in the course of asteroid bombardment.

The reason Dr Olbers was able to predict the existence of this vast belt of rocks is positively scary. He believed there had been a full-sized planet in orbit between Mars and Jupiter at one time and for some reason it had exploded.

At the time most astronomers agreed with him. A few

still do, but today a more popular theory is that the Asteroid Belt was formed, more or less as it is today, at the same time as the rest of the solar system.

87 What's a comet?

The American astronomer Fred L. Whipple famously said it was a dirty snowball.

The name comet is used to describe any object orbiting the sun that develops a glowing gas surround and a luminous tail as it gets close. Comets generally have very long orbits. Our Earth orbits the sun once a year. The most famous comet – Halley's – takes 76 years on average and what are called long-period comets can take hundreds, even thousands of years to complete a single circuit.

If you look at a distant comet through a telescope the only thing you can see is its nucleus, which is what they call the solid part at the centre. For a long time nobody was quite sure what this was made of. Some scientists thought it might be rock, some iron. In 1950, Dr Whipple put forward his dirty-snowball theory, which made a lot of sense to a lot of people and was finally confirmed in 1986 when the *Giotto* spacecraft took close-up photographs of Halley's Comet.

So what you have in a typical comet is a lumpy mass made up of various types of ice, but mainly frozen water just like the ice that forms on ponds in winter. This is mixed up with some sort of fine dust that looks just like soot and may even be soot. (Ninety percent of Halley's ice surface is covered in the black dust.)

Did you know?

The appearance of a comet has long been thought of as a disaster sign, possibly with good reason. Once the ice of the nucleus starts to melt, some of the larger particles will break away to take up their own orbits which will be very similar to the orbit of the comet itself. The result is that the comet begins to trail a meteor stream. If the Earth happens to pass through such a stream, a meteor shower results. Like most meteors, these usually burn out in the upper atmosphere, but it may have been that one or two reached ground zero in the distant past, causing comets to be associated with disastrous events.

Compared to the blazing comet as a whole, the nucleus tends to be quite small. In Halley's Comet, for example, the core is a stretched out lump measuring only about 15 by 8 kilometres (9 by 5 miles). You'd be lucky to spot anything that size with a powerful telescope, yet Halley's Comet is perfectly visible to the naked eye on a clear night. The reason is that when comets approach the sun, something quite spectacular happens.

Once your comet gets to within about three astronomical units (450,000,000 kilometres or 279,000,000 miles) from the sun, the dusty crust starts to heat up. Heat is then transferred into the icy core which begins to vaporise. The gas leaves the comet, carrying some of the dust particles with it. What's produced is a cloud made up mainly of water, but with carbon monoxide, carbon dioxide, methane, ammonia and carbon disulfide as well.

The mixture takes in radiation from the sun and sends it out again on another wavelength. Once that happens, the cloud starts to glow. By the time the comet is within 150,000,000 kilometres (93,000,000 miles) of the sun, the core is surrounded by a vast glowing sphere of gas and dust – called the coma – which can be anything up to 100,000 kilometres (62,000 miles) across.

By this time, something else spectacular is happening as well. The sun generates a stream of particles and radiation known as the 'solar wind'. When the solar wind hits the gas cloud around the comet, it sweeps away ions to form the comet's plasma tail. This will always point away from the sun whichever direction the comet itself is heading.

88 How fast do I have to go to get off the Earth?

What you're asking about here is escape velocity, which scientists define as the speed you need to reach in order to get away from a specific source of gravity (like a planet) without having to accelerate any further.

Calculating escape velocity is trickier than you might think because the farther you move away from the planet the less speed you need to get away from it altogether. This is because the gravitational pull is weakening the farther you go. The boffins have worked out that you can calculate escape velocity at any given distance from a planet by multiplying the speed needed to hold a circular orbit at that height by the square root of two.

No, I can't work that out either, but I'm reliably assured that if you want to get off the Earth, you have to do a little better than 11.2 kilometres (6.96 miles) per second. The figure is the actual escape velocity of our planet, but doesn't take into account our atmosphere, which will always slow you down a bit.

Before you ask, escape velocity on the moon is about 2.4 kilometres (1.4 miles) per second, which makes the return trip a bit easier.

89 Has anybody ever seen a real alien?

There have been rumours…

In 1963, a married couple named Betty and Barney Hill turned up at the offices of a Boston psychiatrist named Benjamin Simon complaining of anxiety and nightmares. They also had memory blanks about a two-hour period while they were returning from a holiday in Montreal, Canada, in 1961.

After examining them both, Dr Simon decided neither had any mental illness. He then used hypnosis to help them remember what had happened during the missing two hours.

Both the Hills reported that on September 19, 1961, while driving back from Canada, they'd seen a strange light in the sky which revealed itself as some sort of flying craft. Barney used binoculars and was able to see alien beings inside it. A little later, their car was flagged down by small, grey humanoid beings with large eyes.

The Hills were taken against their will into the alien spacecraft where they were given a medical examination that included taking skin and hair samples. The aliens 'spoke' to them by telepathy and afterwards ordered them to forget what had happened – which was exactly what they'd done until hypnotised.

Did you know?

Dr John Mack, Professor of Psychiatry at America's Harvard Medical School, has reported that polls and surveys suggest several hundred thousand to several million Americans have experienced abduction by aliens.

Furthermore, in 1947, the American Army Air Force Base at Roswell in New Mexico issued a press release to say the Air Force had retrieved the wreckage of an alien spacecraft that had crashed nearby.

Although the story was quickly withdrawn – Air Force officers decided the wreckage was really a weather balloon – witnesses in the area insist that two alien bodies were found at the crash site and spirited away by the military. Some even claimed that one of the two was still alive and survived for some time afterwards.

90 Who invented the first telescope?

Most of the textbooks say it was Galileo, a famous Italian mathematician who later became more famous still as an astronomer. But the truth is the very first telescope was invented by a Dutch man whose name nobody seems to know any more.

In 1609, Galileo Galilei, a professor of mathematics, was teaching at the University of Padua, in Italy, when a Dutch inventor turned up in the town. The man talked too much. Before long Galileo discovered he was on his way to Venice to demonstrate the benefits of an amazing new optical instrument – the telescope.

Galileo knew a good thing when he saw one. He contacted his friend Paolo Sarpi and asked him to intervene with the Venetian authorities, promising them that Galileo would soon provide them with a far better telescope than anything likely to come out of the Netherlands. The authorities believed him and sent the Dutch inventor packing.

On August 21, the elderly members of the Venetian Senate puffed their way up the bell-tower of their local cathedral to examine Galileo's new 'spy-glass'. They were very impressed indeed. They could see people walking on the distant island of Murano and spot ships approaching the bay long before they could be seen with the naked eye.

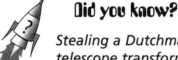

Did you know?

Stealing a Dutchman's idea for the telescope transformed Galileo into the first modern astronomer and brought him lasting fame.

It was those ships that really turned them on. It didn't take a genius to realize that the earlier you could see approaching ships, the better prepared you would be for any attack from the sea. The Senate promptly placed a large order for Galileo's new telescopes.

Galileo himself was struck soon after with the idea of turning a telescope towards the heavens and so discovered several things no-one had ever known before, including the fact that the Milky Way was made from millions of separate stars and the planet Saturn had a ring around it.

Those of you with a sneaking sympathy for the badly treated Dutchman, may take some satisfaction from the fact that Galileo's study of the night sky quickly

Galileo Galilei

convinced him the Earth was not the centre of the universe and was silly enough to say so in a book he wrote in 1629. This so upset the Pope that Galileo was sentenced to death.

When Galileo admitted on his knees that he was wrong, the death sentence was changed to house arrest for life, with the additional penance of having 'Hail Marys' recited at him every day by a nun. Three hundred and fifty years later, in 1992, the Church finally realised Galileo had been right all along and Pope John Paul II apologised for its treatment of him.

91   Why do they call our space telescope the Hubble telescope?

What we're talking about here is one of the wonders of the twentieth century – and the twenty-first come to that.

The biggest problem we have with ordinary astronomical telescopes is that they look up at the stars through a thick layer of atmosphere. This distorts the picture dramatically and in some ways blanks it out altogether. It's as if you were a fish trying to study birds on the basis of the wavy, distorted images you saw as they flew above the water's surface.

In 1977, the United States Congress solved the problem when they gave the green light for the placing of a telescope in space.

The device was a large reflecting telescope attached to two cameras. Its biggest mirror was 239 centimetres across and there were instruments built in that could detect visible, ultraviolet and infrared light. It was capable of detecting objects 50 times fainter than

anything you could see using the largest ground-based telescope and delivering pictures ten times better. It had one spectrograph to tell you the chemical composition of what you were looking at and another to gather ultraviolet light that would never penetrate the Earth's atmosphere.

The space telescope was built under NASA supervision and placed in orbit 600 kilometres (370 miles) above our planet by the crew of the Space Shuttle on April 25, 1990. Almost at once it started to send back some fabulous pictures, but about a month later it became obvious something was wrong. It turned out the main mirror was the wrong shape and there were problems with the gyroscopes that held the scope's position and the solar arrays that fed it power.

In December 1993, Shuttle astronauts undertook five space walks to replace defective parts and install additional mirrors to correct the fault in the main one. The mission worked like a charm and the pictures the telescope has sent back since then are the finest images from space you will ever see.

They call it the Hubble Telescope because it was

named after American Edwin Hubble, one of the foremost astronomers of recent times.

92 What's a radio telescope?

Forget any pictures in your head of a tube with lenses. A radio telescope is an instrument used by astronomers that consists of a receiver attached to an antenna or dish used to pick up radio signals from beyond our planet. The first one was built in 1937 by an American astronomer named Grote Reber.

Because radio waves are a lot longer than light waves, radio telescopes have to be a lot bigger than optical telescopes to achieve the same sort of results. The largest in the world, 16 kilometres (10 miles) south of Arecibo in Puerto Rico, completely fills a natural bowl-shaped depression some 305 metres in diameter. Among the things it's done so far is map the surface of Venus.

But Arecibo is only the world's largest *single* radio telescope. Astronomers are now building them in linked arrays. This means large numbers of smallish dishes arranged over a large area – like the 27-antenna Very

Large Array near Socorro, New Mexico – can pull in signals equivalent to single dishes so large we could never actually build them.

93 Who was the first astronomer?

The first one in the modern sense was Galileo since before him anybody studying the stars had to do so without the benefit of a telescope.

However, people were studying the stars long before Galileo's day, right back to Ancient Egypt, Sumeria and beyond, so the name of the very first astronomer is lost.

94 How can I get a galaxy named after me?

Change your name to 'M' by deed poll. Galaxies are named as M followed by a number in the most popular star catalogue used by amateur astronomers. The M stands for Messier, after Charles Messier, the French astronomer who compiled the catalogue in the eighteenth century, having discovered a great many of its galaxies himself. Within this catalogue, the M1 is the Crab Nebula, while Andromeda is the M31.

Your other shot is to change your name to NGC, plus a high number. The NGC – New General Catalogue – is the one professional astronomers generally use nowadays.

95 What about a star then?

Although there are about 5,000 stars visible to the naked eye, only a few hundred have been named, so the rest are up for grabs. This fact has not gone unnoticed by commercial companies who offer to name a star after you, record it in their star catalogue and send you a map of the sky with your star highlighted.

Nothing wrong with that, of course, but it won't get your name into the star catalogues the professional astronomers use.

To be honest, star names are a bit of a mess. Some, like Procyon and Canopis, come more or less directly from the Greek. The ones that start with 'Al' like Algol or Aldebaran were usually named by the Arabs (who named most of the stars that have proper names). A handful come from the Latin.

You do get some proper star names that are comparatively recent, like Cor Caroli, named in 1725 by Edmond Halley, but nowadays it's all letters and numbers tied in to the particular catalogue used, sometimes with the star's right ascension (a reference to its position) tagged on. So the star Vega can also be called (are you ready for this?) HD 172167 or GC 25466 or ADS 11510 or even BD +38°3238.

But that's just ordinary stars. Variable stars are a little nightmare all of their own. They're named in the order of their discovery within a given constellation by the letters R to Z, providing they don't already have a Greek letter. If you run out of letters, you go back to R and double it. This will take you all the way to ZZ, after which you go to AA and run all the way to AZ, then BB to BZ and so on, leaving out the letter J for some reason. If you run out of letters completely, you jump to V335, V336, V337, continuing until the cows come home.

I really wouldn't want to be named after a star if you paid me.

96 Any chance of a planet?

No chance.

In 1781 when William Herschel discovered a seventh planet, he named it 'Georgium Sidus' in honour of King George III. His colleagues in the astronomical community were having none of it. They changed the name to 'Herschel' after Herschel himself, but even that didn't stick. Before long the new planet had been renamed Uranus in the classical tradition that insists planets must be called after gods.

So if even the astronomer who discovers a new planet doesn't have the final say in what it's called, the possibility of having a planet called after you are slim.

Unless you become a god, of course.

it's Quiz time!

5

This one should be easy — it's mainly about the planet you live on, right? Answer the questions, check your answers, keep your score.

1 Who headed the first voyage to sail right around the world?

2 What's the Earth's core made of?

3 Name the world's biggest space rocket.

4 Who calculated the Roche Limit?

5 What is escape velocity on the moon in kilometres per second?

6 Roughly how many stars are visible to the naked eye?

7 Where's the largest radio telescope in the world?

8 What part of the Hubble Telescope gave trouble after it was placed in orbit in 1990?

9 Where did the US Air Force claim (then later deny) they'd found the wreckage of a flying saucer?

10 What nationality was the scientist who discovered the Mohorovicic discontinuity?

97 Can we beam up to space ships like they do in *Star Trek?*

Not yet, and possibly not ever. There are real problems with the physics involved in *Star Trek* beam-ups.

A beam-up is one version of something known as matter transmission and the technicalities involved hardly bear thinking about. The basic problem is that as you sit enraptured by this book, you are composed of 100,000,000,000,000,000,000,000,000,000,000 atoms. (That's a hundred thousand billion, billion – and big hefty British billions at that.) Every last one of them fits into its own specific place in a hideously complicated pattern making up the attractive and delightful person you are.

Once you realize that, you begin to get some idea of the problems involved in beaming anywhere. You have to be broken down into your constituent atoms and each of those hundred thousand billion billion atoms has to be transmitted to your destination. You have to make sure no atoms are lost and you have to reassemble every one of the hundred thousand billion billion in exactly the right order. The results of even the slightest mistake could be catastrophic.

But let's suppose you decide to try. The first thing you have to do is break yourself down into your most basic particles, which means overcoming the energy that holds you together at the sub-atomic level. The only way we know how to do that is heat you up to 1,000,000,000,000 degrees. The energy needed to do so is equivalent to a 100 megaton H-bomb.

Did you know?

Despite all the apparent difficulties, Australian scientists announced in 2002 that they had succeeded in the instantaneous transfer of light particles (photons) from one side of the laboratory to the other – the first-ever example of a technology that might beam you up one day.

To transmit matter the way you might transmit a radio signal – which is what they do in *Star Trek* – you have to pump up the particles to somewhere close to the speed of light. This requires 10 times more energy than you used to break them down in the first place.

Put those two requirements together and you need about 10,000 times more power for a single transportation than is currently consumed at any given moment in every country throughout the entire world. And that's not counting the power needed to put the particles back together again. Since we've no idea how to do that, we don't know how much it will add to the electricity bill.

One way around all this daunting power consumption is to use the principle of the fax machine. When you fax a document half way around the world, the actual paper doesn't go anywhere. All you send is the information, which allows the receiving machine to create an exact copy of your message at the destination.

Some scientists think it might be possible one day to scan you and record the exact composition and position of every atom in your body. Transmitting this information would take a lot less power than transmitting the matter itself. When the information reached the beam-up receiving station, it could be used to duplicate you exactly.

Unfortunately this approach has a drawback as well. It means that suddenly there are two of you – one standing patiently at the sending station, the other newly created at the receiving station. Since it's confusing being in two places at once, the original you would have to be destroyed. Thus any beam-up machine has to take into account the same problem criminals face when they murder somebody – what to do with the body.

If beam-ups became even half as popular as airline travel, the duplicate corpses would be piled sky high.

98 How about travelling at warp speed?

This one's really tricky.

When you watch *Star Trek,* the *Enterprise* goes into warp and travels several light years in a few minutes.

Which means the starship has (somehow) gone faster than the speed of light.

Now the first thing to say about that is you can't take something flying at a few thousand or even a few hundred thousand kilometres per hour and accelerate it so it eventually goes faster than the speed of light. There are three reasons for this, all of which were worked out by Albert Einstein a long time ago.

The first is technical. To push a rocket anywhere near the speed of light requires more fuel than you can carry in a rocket. And that's not just the fuel we use today, but any sort of fuel we might imagine using in the future. The energy needed to get the *Enterprise* up to a useful percentage of light speed is just too high.

The other two have to do with the laws of physics. Einstein's calculations showed that if you forget about technical considerations and imagine you can somehow speed up the ship, a very nasty situation develops.

First, time slows down the faster you go. At first this is hardly noticeable, but as you approach the speed of light, time really does go slower and slower. When you reach the speed of light, it stops. And when you go faster than the speed of light, time goes into reverse.

Did you know?

Faster-than-light travel has various drawbacks, not least of which is the fact that it involves moving backwards in time.

It's very difficult to get your head around what that might mean if you were simply trying to make a trip to

Sirius. But fortunately you don't have to, because there's something else that comes into play to make sure you don't travel faster than light.

As your speed builds, not only does time slow down, but the mass of your spaceship and everything in it increases. When you reach the speed of light, the mass of your ship becomes infinite. So before you pass the light-speed barrier, the *Enterprise* is so massive it fills the entire universe.

Put all these things together and you can see why Einstein told his fellow scientists you could never accelerate a solid body to exceed the speed of light. You can also see why they believed him.

The people behind *Star Trek* believed him too. If you pay close attention you'll notice Kirk, Picard, Janeway and the rest never talk about faster-than-light travel. They talk about warp travel. And while warp may get you from here to there faster than light does, it never actually involves *travelling* faster than light. It involves distorting space.

Imagine space is like the surface of the sea and you're popping along in your outboard at four knots trying to reach an island seven kilometres (4 miles) away. At your present rate of speed, that's going to take you an hour.

Now imagine a massive wave builds up behind you travelling at 60 km/h (37 mph). The wave picks up your little boat and sweeps it along towards the island. Just seven minutes later, it's deposited you on the beach. But your boat, on top of the wave, never increased its speed. The outboard kept running at a steady four knots. Yet you reached your destination in a fraction of the time it would normally have taken.

That's one way you might imagine warp drive working. It creates a 'wave in space' which carries you along towards a distant destination without your having to increase your speed.

Another way would be to imagine warp drive bends the space between your starting point and your destination, so that the two are temporarily closer together. Once again, you can make the journey faster without actually increasing your speed.

But can space really be distorted? The answer is a definite yes. The gravitational field of a Black Hole distorts the space around it. So, to a lesser extent, does the gravity of a neutron star – as does any source of gravity, although the effect is scarcely measurable with less massive objects.

All of which brings us to the bottom line of your question which is this.

We don't have a warp drive yet. We don't even have the slightest idea how we might build one. But unlike faster-than-light travel, a warp drive doesn't contradict the laws of physics as we understand them.

99 What are flying saucers?

Back in 1947, an American pilot named Kenneth Arnold

was on a search mission for a crashed transport plane. He was flying his single-engined aircraft over Mount Rainier in Washington State when he saw nine disc-shaped objects fly past him in two parallel lines.

They didn't look like any aircraft he knew or, indeed, anything else that should have been up there. Mr Arnold used a method known as triangulation to calculate their speed and came up with a figure of 2574.4 km/h (1,600 mph) – way above anything the fastest plane could manage at that time.

When a bewildered Arnold landed and reported the strange sighting, he described the discs as moving 'like a saucer would if you skipped it across the water.' Newspapers latched on to this colourful description at once and headlined the discs as 'flying saucers.'

Kenneth Arnold's experience was the start of something big. Since 1947, flying saucers – or Unidentified Flying Objects (UFOs) – have been reported in virtually every country of the world. It even transpires that they were about before Arnold reported them. During World War Two, which ended in 1945, pilots on both sides of the conflict reported 'foo fighters' – flying discs usually believed to be enemy secret aircraft. Historically, there are drawings of flying saucers in medieval manuscripts, reports of UFOs from Ancient Rome and even representations on rock art dating to prehistoric times. They were described in ancient Hindu religious epics like the *Ramayana*.

Government scientists have generally dismissed flying saucers as hallucinations or mistaken identifications of things like weather balloons, ball lightning or the planet Venus. Others who have studied the reports conclude they are space ships visiting Earth from an alien civilization, vehicles from another dimension or reality, or even timeships which originated in our distant future.

100 What's NASA?

The letters stand for **N**ational **A**eronautics and **S**pace **A**dministration. It's an American government agency set up in 1958 to develop space exploration following the Soviet launch of the first artificial Earth satellite (*Sputnik*) the year before.

NASA has its headquarters in Washington, DC and is affiliated to several major research centres, including the Jet Propulsion Laboratory in Pasadena, California, and the Lyndon B. Johnson Space Center in Houston, Texas. It was responsible for the Apollo Program that put a man on the moon in 1969 and is currently working towards a manned Mars landing over the next decade or so.

It also has some really cool websites. Your best jumping-off place to see them is at http://www.nasa.gov.

101 If somebody from another planet visited the Earth, would we kill him?

Humanity has a long, painful history of killing things we don't understand, so the chances are we would, although it probably depends where he or she landed.

If it was anywhere in the developed West, we'd almost certainly lock him up somewhere nice and private, conduct nasty experiments to find out about his internal organs and back-engineer his spaceship so we could profit from the technology. My bet is he'd die in captivity.

If it was somewhere 'primitive', like a tribal community in a rainforest, he might be kept as a pet if he looked cute or hunted for meat if he didn't.

If he landed in a war zone – and there will be several wars going on somewhere in the world whenever you happen to be reading this – we'd probably shoot him without even noticing.

But all that supposes he's a gentle, helpless sort of alien who arrives in a spirit of peace and good will. If he was a really tough alien with advanced weapons technology, we'd try to take him out with something brutal like an H-bomb and if that didn't work, we'd worship him, or her, as a god.

102 Could I drink fizzy lemonade in a space station?

Wouldn't advise it. Coping with liquids in the zero-gravity confines of a space station is a very tricky business. They don't pour, so you have to squeeze them out of a squeezy bottle. The liquid then hangs there in a great globule and you have to suck it in to drink it.

I've actually no idea what carbonisation (fizz) would do to that globule, but I'd hate to find out.

103 Where's the hottest place in the solar system?

The centre of the sun, which has a temperature of about 15,000,000°K (14,726,850°C).

104 And what about the coldest?

That would be the surface of Pluto, the outermost planet of the solar system. It's covered in methane ice and indications are that in places the temperature drops to a chilly 35°K, equivalent to –238°C.

105 Do men or women make the best astronauts?

Although most astronauts to date have been men, anybody with half a brain can see women are better equipped for the job. They're generally smaller so they take up less room in a spacecraft. They're generally lighter, so it requires less fuel to get them off the planet. And because their bodies evolved to cope with childbirth, they're generally more physically and emotionally resilient than men.

So how come most astronauts to date have been men? Ask NASA.

106 Have we ever sent women into space?

Yes. The first woman to travel into space was Valentina Tereshkova, a Soviet cosmonaut. In the summer of 1963, she climbed aboard the spacecraft *Vostok 6* and blasted off to make 48 orbits of our planet over the next 71 hours. Strangely enough she had no pilot training, but she was an enthusiastic amateur parachutist and this was enough to get her into the Russian Cosmonaut Programme in 1961.

Although Ms Tereshkova performed her duties admirably and the trip was a complete success except for a bout of space sickness, there was a long gap before a woman was again permitted to make a space trip. In 1982, Svetlana Savitskaya, another Soviet cosmonaut, also went into orbit.

The Americans caught up the following year when Sally Kristen Ride became the first American woman in space. She took a six-day trip as flight engineer in the Space Shuttle *Challenger*. In 1984, she completed a second space mission, accompanied by her friend Kathryn Sullivan who became the first American woman to undertake a space walk.

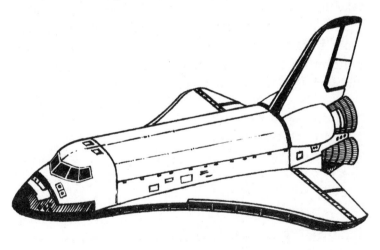

More recently, astronaut Eileen Collins became the first woman to pilot a Space Shuttle. In February 1995, she flew *Discovery* to rendezvous with the Russian space station Mir. Two years later, she was back in the pilot's seat for an actual docking with Mir in which personnel, equipment and supplies were transferred to the space station. In March 1999, she was named the world's first woman shuttle commander. By then she had more than 400 hours in-space experience under her belt.

107 What happens on a space walk?

You put on a space suit and go outside your spaceship or space station, usually to make some sort of repairs.

It's an interesting experience, by all accounts. Since you're outside the Earth's gravity, there's not much of a sensation of up or down. There's no horizon or familiar landmark, except for your craft and maybe the bulk of your planet, which hangs in space above or below you (whichever you decide).

You're tethered to the craft to stop you floating off into space and you get from here to there either with the aid of a small jet-pack or by pulling yourself along using any hand-holds you can find.

You're in a silent world except for any radio chatter over the earphones in your helmet and most directions you look you can see forever. If anything punctures your suit you're in big trouble.

108 Why do you need a space suit?

Two reasons. There's no air in the vacuum of space, so without a space suit you couldn't breathe. But even more importantly, without air there's no air pressure, which is something that would make you forget your breathing problems very quickly. You never notice it, but you spend your life on Earth with the weight of the

atmosphere pressing down on you. Take that away – which is what would happen if you ventured from your craft into space without a suit – and the internal pressures of your body would cause it to swell and burst like a balloon, only more messily.

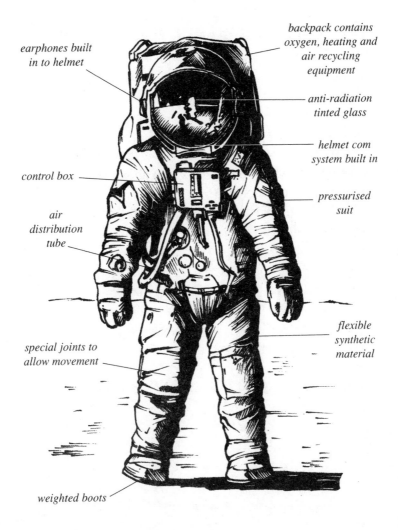

earphones built in to helmet

backpack contains oxygen, heating and air recycling equipment

anti-radiation tinted glass

helmet com system built in

control box

pressurised suit

air distribution tube

flexible synthetic material

special joints to allow movement

weighted boots

109 Could you sail a ship in space?

Yes, oddly enough. Nobody's made one yet, but a space yacht is a definite design possibility, at least inside the solar system.

What makes it a possibility is the solar wind, a constant stream of particles emitted by the sun. The solar wind moves at speeds of 350 to 700 kilometres (217 to 435 miles) per second, and extends as far as Neptune.

A small craft with a large sail – say 1.6 kilometres (1 mile) or more square – could trap the solar wind exactly the same way sailing ships do with winds blowing across the terrestrial oceans.

A sail that size would be impossible on Earth, but becomes feasible in the zero gravity of space.

110 Have people died in space?

Sadly, quite a few.

Vladimir Mikhaylovich Komarov, a Soviet cosmonaut, was the first person to die during a space mission. Komarov became a pilot in 1949 and in 1964 was chosen to fly *Voskhod 1*, the first craft to carry more than one human being into space. That one came down safely and three years later, flying alone this time, he blasted into orbit in *Soyuz 1*.

Everything seemed fine until he tried to land again after 18 circuits of the globe. Then something went wrong several kilometres up and the craft crashed. Komarov was killed and his ashes are now entombed in a wall of the Kremlin in Moscow.

You might argue that Komarov didn't actually die in space, although it was a space mission that killed him.

But there's no such doubt about three other Soviet cosmonauts who perished in 1971. Mission commander Georgy T. Dobrovolsky, flight engineer Vladislav N. Volkov and design engineer Viktor Ivanovich Patsayev flew their *Soyuz 11* craft to make a successful docking with the Salyut space station launched into orbit two months earlier.

They set a world record at the time by remaining in space for 24 days, after which their recovery capsule made a perfect landing in Kazakstan. But when the capsule was opened, all three were dead. They had perished in space, probably somewhere high over Iran, when their air leaked away after a hatch door failed to close properly.

The Soviets weren't the only ones to lose good people to their space programme. In February 1967, the Americans were simulating a launch of their *Apollo 1* spacecraft when a flash fire swept through the capsule killing all three occupants, Virgil I. Grissom, Edward H. White II and Roger B. Chaffee.

But maybe the most tragic space programme death of all was that of Christa Corrigan McAuliffe, an American schoolteacher chosen out of thousands to become the first civilian to make the trip into space.

Ms McAuliffe joined the crew of the Space Shuttle *Challenger* in 1986. After some delays, the launch finally took place at 11.38 a.m. on January 28. One minute and 13 seconds later, the craft exploded high above the Atlantic. There were no survivors.

111 Why don't people live in space?

The main problem's gravity – or rather the lack of it.

You never think about it, but every minute of every day of your life, you've been subject to the gravitational pull of an entire planet – the Earth you were born on. Your body has been developed to withstand that pull and if you take it away, you would miss it.

It won't do you any harm to find yourself in zero gravity for an hour or two, but if your stay is prolonged to as little as a week or more, your muscles begin to waste away. The longer you stay, the more the wastage; and if you don't do something about it, you'll die.

What you have to do about it is exercise. A strict, regular, exercise regime will keep your muscles trim and your body healthy. But most people just don't have the time to exercise enough, so the idea of building an orbiting housing estate is unlikely to catch on in the immediate future.

Did you know?

For a prolonged stay in space you would have to exercise for eight hours or more a day, every day, until you came back down again.

That said, some people – most of them Russians – have lived in space for quite prolonged periods of time. Towards the end of February 1986, what was then the Soviet Union launched the core module of its Mir space station, a housing unit of sorts designed to accommodate one or two hardy astronauts prepared to spend real living time in space.

And spend it they did. The first occupants of Mir were Leonid Kizim and Vladimir Solovyev – the Russians call them cosmonauts rather than astronauts – who spent 53 days up there. In 1987 a record of 326 consecutive days in space was set by a Mir crewman, only to be broken the following year by two others who stayed a total of 366 days. But the world champ in this department is a cosmonaut named Valery Polyakov who came home on March 22, 1995 after spending 438 days in space.

These remarkable feats show living in space can certainly be done – it just isn't easy. But despite the difficulties, there are people convinced it's going to happen on a large scale one day. Among them is the American astronaut Buzz Aldrin, the second man to walk on the moon. Aldrin is one member of a scientific business team who have submitted a detailed plan to NASA to build a chain of orbiting hotels between Earth and Mars.

Mir

The first unit could be in place as early as 2018, with two more to follow over the next four years. The idea is to provide temporary accommodation for colonists en route to Mars.

At the moment, the only time it makes sense to fly to Mars is when the orbits of Mars and Earth bring the two planets close together. But with Buzz Aldrin's units in place, you could head for the Red Planet any time and simply stop off at the orbiting hotel until Mars came close enough for you to continue your journey.

it's **Quiz** time!

Last of our quizzes coming up. Answer the questions, check your answers just as you've done before, then move on to find out how you did overall.

1   Where are NASA headquarters?

2   How fast does the solar wind blow?

3   Which American astronaut plans to build hotels in space?

4   Where have the first steps in 'beam-me-up' technology been taken?

5   If you could travel faster than light where would you go?

6   What covers the surface of Pluto?

7   What is the common name for UFOs?

8   Roughly how many atoms are there in your body?

9   What's the problem with drinking in space?

10 How many Earth orbits did cosmonaut Komarov make before he was killed?

Answers

1. Washington, DC
2. Anywhere between 350 and 700 km (217 and 435 miles) per second
3. Buzz Aldrin 4. Australia 5. Back in time 6. Methane ice
7. Flying saucers
8. A hundred thousand billion, give or take a few
9. Lack of gravity 10. 18

How do you rate as a
SpaceQuest Expert?

You've answered the questions and kept note of your scores. Now add the scores together to find out how many answers you got right in all the quizzes put together. Then check your rating in the table below:

Number of Correct Answers	Rating
10 or fewer	Waste of Space
11 to 20	Useless Worm
21 to 30	Budding Astronomer
31 to 40	Eye on the Sky
41 to 50	Cunning Observer
51 to 59	Master of the Universe
60	Godlike Superentity

Index